MW01714204

Wasteland Scavenging Operations

A Zombie Apocalypse Field Manual

JP Wilder

Edge Weaver LLC

Wasteland Scavenging Operations
A Zombie Apocalypse Field Manual

Edge Weaver Fantasy & Adventure is an imprint of Edge Weaver LLC

Book Design: Marie Pitrat

Kindle ISBN: 978-1-964406-34-3

Paperback ISBN: 978-1-964406-35-0

Published in the United States of America

Edge Weaver LLC
19360 Rinaldi #681
Porter Ranch, CA 91326-1607

Contents

Preface

Welcome, survivor, to the most indispensable guide you'll never actually need: a *Field Manual for Scavenging Operations During the Zombie Apocalypse*. If you've ever feared a moan in the dark or that a shuffle behind the bushes might be something more sinister than your neighbor walking their dog, then you, my friend, have picked up the right book.

Now, you might ask, "Is this serious?" The short answer: No. The slightly longer answer: Absolutely not, but we'll have a lot of fun pretending it is. This manual is a blend of survival tactics, strategic musings, and outright absurdity, tailored for the enthusiast of the undead, the lover of the post-apocalyptic genre, and anyone who's ever wondered if they could outrun their friend when chased by a horde of zombies.

Why a Zombie Survival Manual?

Why focus on zombies in a world teeming with survival manuals for every disaster, from earthquakes to alien invasions? Zombies capture our imagination like nothing else—the slow creeping dread of the undead, the collapse of society, the challenge of surviving against the odds. Plus, preparing for zombies is a lot more exciting than preparing for a power outage.

This manual is thus crafted for two purposes. First, it entertains and engages your imagination with scenarios that spark creativity and laughter. Second, it offers a parody-laced look at real survival strategies—yes, beneath the veneer of zombie lore, you'll find actual tactics that might just come in handy during less undead emergencies.

Navigating This Manual

You can approach this manual in one of two ways. If you're the methodical type, you might start at the beginning and work your way through each meticulously crafted chapter, absorbing every tip and tactic to build your survival skills in a logical order. Alternatively, you might dive straight into whatever chapter catches your fancy—whether it's learning about the best formations for patrolling zombie-infested territories or figuring out how to perform a silent takedown on a zombie that used to be a door-to-door salesman.

Each chapter is designed to build on the one before. That said, you may jump in at any point and still understand the key points made in the manual without feeling lost. Still, a sequential journey might offer a more immersive experience, helping you build a comprehensive survival strategy as you go.

The Tone and Humor of the Apocalypse

This manual does not shy away from humor. In fact, it embraces it with the fervor of a zombie spotting a slow-moving meal. The apocalypse, for all its doom and gloom, needs a bit of levity and what better way to provide this than through a guide that takes itself seriously in the art of not being serious at all?

Engagement and Imagination

As you peruse these pages, I encourage you to fully engage with the content. Imagine your neighborhood as a series of strategic zones—where would you set up defenses? What local resources could you exploit? Who in your community would make the best members of your survival squad?

Consider this manual as a conversation starter. Share it with friends and debate the best ways to outmaneuver a horde or laugh over which zombie movie characters would have definitely benefited from this guide.

Summary and Conclusion

Before you turn the page and step bravely into a world besieged by the walking dead, remember: the goal of this manual is to prepare you for everything and nothing all at once. It's about embracing the absurdity of life (and undeath), exploring the "what ifs," and having a great time doing it.

So, strap on your backpack, arm yourself with whatever gardening tools seem most menacing, and prepare to delve into the art of surviving the zombie apocalypse—not because you need to, but because why wouldn't you want to?

Case Study

This manual shows extended examples from a real-life mission carried out by a group of zombie apocalypse survivors known as Sierra's Crew. This will showcase how the tactics, procedures, and best practices discussed can be effectively implemented in the field against the very real threat of the undead.

The Battle of Quarryville: *This harrowing operation will follow Sierra's team as they execute a scavenging mission to resupply vital medical resources from an abandoned depot. Despite careful planning and recon, the mission runs into nearly disastrous consequences when they attract the attention of a massive zombie horde.*

You will see firsthand the importance of recon, establishing security overwatch and fields of fire, battle tracking and reacting to contingencies, and following an organized break-away and exfiltration plan when the scavenging site is overrun.

By analyzing the decisions, actions, and lessons learned by Sierra's Crew over the course of this mission, you can gain a deeper understanding of how to properly apply and handle the scavenging, recon, and survival principles covered in this manual.

So, keep an eye out for these case study insets as you learn the fundamentals. Sierra's Crew's real-life experiences will make the teachings memorable and drive home the grave consequences of disregarding them when the undead arrive.

Introduction

1.0 Welcome to the Apocalypse

Welcome, brave survivor! If you've ever chuckled nervously at a creaking door or rehearsed your escape route from the grocery store, you're in the right place. This manual isn't just about surviving a zombie apocalypse—it's about thriving in the chaos with a smile. Why zombies? Because if you can survive the undead, a regular Tuesday is nothing.

1.1 The Rise of the Zombies

Zombies have shambled their way through our nightmares and into our hearts. From classic horror films to modern-day blockbusters, these creatures represent the ultimate survival challenge. They're relentless, numerous, and, let's face it, culturally fascinating. This manual taps into that undead obsession, blending survivalist tactics with the thrills of the zombie genre.

1.2 Overview of the Manual's Structure

You're embarking on a journey through seven meticulously crafted chapters, each designed to prepare you for anything the apocalypse throws your way:

Chapter 2: Understanding the Zombie Threat
Chapter 3: Scavenging Essentials
Chapter 4: Pre-operation Scouting and Planning
Chapter 5: Effective Scavenge Operations
Chapter 6: Survival and Exfiltration to Base
Chapter 7: Conclusion

Each section builds on the last, turning you from a nervous novice into a confident survivor.

1.3 What You Will Learn

By the end of this manual, you'll have mastered the art of zombie evasion and the skills necessary to lead a group of survivors on a mission to procure food, gear, and supplies. We'll delve into strategies to maintain security, find the loot, and lead the people that you will need to rely on in order to survive in a world overrun by walkers.

1.4 Navigating the Manual

Dive in sequentially to build your knowledge base step-by-step or jump directly to topics of immediate interest.

1.5 The Importance of Humor in Survival

Laughter isn't just the best medicine; it's your best friend in times of crisis. It reduces stress, boosts morale, and can even diffuse tense situations, making it an essential survival tool.

1.6 Summary and Conclusion

You're not just reading a manual; you're writing your own survival story. As you turn each page, imagine yourself mastering the skills that could one day turn a dire situation into a manageable adventure. So lace up your boots, strap on your backpack, and let's step bravely into a world where being undead is just another hurdle to overcome.

Understanding the Zombie Threat

In the unforgiving wasteland of the post-apocalyptic world, survival hinges on your ability to understand and navigate the dangers posed by the undead. This chapter will delve deeper into the different types of zombies, their behavior patterns, and how to identify danger zones, equipping you with the knowledge and skills necessary to scavenge for food and resources in the wasteland.

2.1. Types of Zombies

In the desolate landscape of the post-apocalyptic world, you will encounter various types of zombies, each presenting its own set of challenges and dangers.

2.1.1 Slow Movers ("Shufflers")

Their sluggish movements and lackluster agility characterize these zombies. They are often seen dragging their feet with minimal coordination. Skin color tends to be pale and mottled, with a distinct odor of decay accompanying their presence.

Combat Strategies: Maintain a safe distance and use ranged weapons. Outmaneuvering shufflers is easy, allowing for effective headshots. In close quarters, firm barricades or simple push barriers will keep them at bay. They exhibit no reaction to water and move slower in cold weather, making them more manageable in freezing climates. Shufflers do not retain any personality traits of their undead hosts; they are driven solely by the primal urge to feed.

Appearance: Typically found in urban areas or places with dense populations. They may wander aimlessly or congregate in large groups.

Attack Style: Often attack head-on because of their slow movements but can be stealthy in quiet environments.

Tracking/Identification: Easily recognizable by their sluggish and uncoordinated movements. They can be tracked by their distinctive footprints and the sound of their dragging feet.

Numbers: Shufflers are commonly found in moderate to large numbers, especially in urban environments where they may form massive hordes.

2.1.2 Sprinters ("Roadrunners")

Unlike their slower brethren, Sprinters can burst into high-speed chases, making them a formidable threat in open areas. They may appear to be human at first, but their skin may appear pale or flushed, with a faint scent of decay. Sprinters react aggressively to fire and may avoid water obstacles unless provoked or pursuing prey. They move faster in cold weather, with their enhanced metabolism providing them with increased energy. There is no evidence to suggest that Sprinters retain any personality traits from their former lives; they operate purely on instinct.

Appearance: Often found in open areas or areas with clear sightlines. They may roam alone or in small groups.

Attack Style: They prefer head-on attacks, relying on their speed to overwhelm their prey.

Tracking/Identification: Sprinters can be identified by their fast and erratic movements. Their approach may be detected by the sound of their rapid footsteps.

Numbers: Sprinters are typically encountered in small to moderate groups, as their speed allows them to cover large distances quickly.

2.1.3 Behemoths ("Tanks")

These towering giants possess a resilience and strength far superior to average zombies. Their presence is typically marked by a distinct, thunderous growl and heavy footsteps. Behemoths often retain some muscle mass, giving their skin a slightly healthier appearance compared to other zombies. They are attracted to water sources but move slower when submerged, making aquatic environments potential safe zones. Behemoths exhibit no personality traits of their former selves; they are driven solely by a primal hunger for flesh.

Combat Strategies: Team coordination is crucial. Use heavy weaponry and incendiary devices to target the head. In the absence of firepower, lead Behemoths into prepared traps or heavy environmental hazards like collapsing structures.

Appearance: Rarely encountered because of their size and slow movements. They may be found in isolated areas or as leaders of zombie hordes.

Attack Style: Behemoths use brute force, charging head-on to overwhelm their targets.

Tracking/Identification: Their distinct growls and heavy footsteps make Behemoths easy to identify. They leave a trail of destruction in their wake, making tracking relatively straightforward.

Numbers: Behemoths are usually encountered singly or in small groups, as their size limits their mobility and ability to travel in large numbers.

2.1.4 Exploders ("Bombers")

These volatile zombies appear distended and unstable, prone to explode upon significant impact, releasing deadly shrapnel. Their skin may appear stretched and discolored, with visible signs of decomposition. Exploders are highly reactive to fire and may explode upon contact with flames, making them a dangerous threat in incendiary environments. They move slower in cold weather, their volatile nature subdued by lower temperatures. Exploders exhibit no personality traits of their former selves; they are driven solely by the urge to self-destruct and cause harm.

Combat Strategies: Engagement from a long range is advised. Sharpshooters should aim for non-critical body parts to trigger detonation from a safe distance. Always move quickly to evade the blast radius post-detonation.

Appearance: Found sporadically among other types of zombies, often in areas with high concentrations of organic matter or debris.

Attack Style: Exploders may attempt to close the distance with their targets before detonating, making stealthy approaches dangerous.

Tracking/Identification: Identifying Exploders can be challenging due to their nondescript appearance. Look for signs of distention or unusual bulges on their bodies.

Numbers: Exploders are typically encountered in small numbers, as their explosive nature makes them a liability in large groups.

2.1.5 Gas Giants ("Hazmats")

Description: Recognizable by their bloated forms and the hazardous gases they emit upon being ruptured, these zombies pose a chemical threat. Their skin appears swollen and discolored, leaking noxious gases when punctured. Gas Giants exhibit no reaction to fire and are drawn to water sources due to their increased buoyancy. They move slower in cold weather, their gaseous emissions becoming more sluggish in lower temperatures. Gas Giants exhibit no personality traits of their former selves; they are driven solely by the urge to spread their toxic emissions.

Combat Strategies: Gas masks or respirators are mandatory. Engage these Hazmats with projectile weapons to avoid direct contact. If indoors, ensure proper ventilation or evacuate to prevent gas accumulation.

Appearance: Found in areas contaminated by hazardous materials or chemical spills. They may be encountered singly or in small groups.

Attack Style: Gas Giants rely on their toxic emissions to incapacitate their prey, making direct confrontation dangerous without proper protection.

Tracking/Identification: Their bloated appearance and the noxious gases they emit make Gas Giants easy to identify. Look for signs of chemical contamination in the surrounding area.

Numbers: Gas Giants are typically encountered in small numbers due to the limited availability of hazardous materials.

2.1.6 Skinnies ("Creepers")

Description: These zombies are more agile and skeletal, using surprise attacks by hiding in dark corners or under debris. Their skin appears tight over their bones, with a faint smell of decay emanating from their bodies. Skinnies are highly sensitive to water, slowing down significantly when wet. They move faster in cold weather due to their sturdier bones in freezing temperatures. Skinnies have no remaining personality from their past lives; they are solely driven by the instinct to hunt and feed.

Combat Strategies: Conduct thorough sweeps of all operational areas with flashlights and thermal or night vision equipment. Have close combat weapons for surprises.

Appearance: Found in covered areas like abandoned buildings or dense forests, often alone or in small groups.

Attack Style: Skinnies prefer sneaky ambushes, attacking from hidden spots to catch prey off guard.

Tracking/Identification: Difficult to spot due to their skeletal appearance and love for shadows. Look for movement or disruptions in the surroundings.

Numbers: Typically encountered in smaller groups as they struggle to coordinate larger attacks because of their stealthy tactics.

2.2 Behavior Patterns

Zombies, by their nature, are unpredictable creatures. However, certain patterns can be identified in their behavior through observation and analysis. Understanding these patterns can greatly increase your chances of survival in the wasteland.

2.2.1 Basic Instincts

At their core, zombies are driven by three basic instincts: hunger, fear, and reproduction.

Hunger: Zombies have an insatiable appetite for human flesh. They will relentlessly pursue any potential food source and will not stop until they are either killed or have fed.

Fear: Zombies are afraid of nothing except fire. When confronted with a large flame or a burning object, they will either retreat or attempt to extinguish the fire.

Reproduction: While zombies do not possess the capability for sexual reproduction, they reproduce in a different manner: through infection. Any living being bitten by a zombie is at risk of becoming infected and turning into one themselves.

2.2.2 Group Dynamics

Zombies tend to gather in groups called hordes. These hordes can range from small clusters to massive swarms of hundreds or even thousands of zombies. The size of the horde depends on various factors, such as the availability of food sources and ease of movement in the area.

Within these hordes, individual zombies exhibit pack mentality and will often cooperate to take down larger prey or overcome obstacles. This makes it dangerous to underestimate even a seemingly small group of zombies.

2.2.3 Environmental Adaptations

Zombies have shown some adaptations to their environment that can affect their behavior. Some of these adaptations are below:

Temperature: As mentioned before, gas giants move slower in colder weather, while skinnies move faster.

Terrain: Zombies are surprisingly adept at navigating different types of terrain, such as forests or urban environments. However, they do encounter difficulties with certain obstacles, such as climbing walls or crossing bodies of water.

2.2.4 Attraction to Sound

Sound is a powerful tool in the fight against zombies. However, it must be used strategically and sparingly to avoid attracting unwanted attention. Zombies are drawn to noise like moths to a flame, their sole purpose being to track down any potential food source. This can quickly lead to swarming behavior and put survivors at risk.

Examples of sounds that can attract zombies include gunshots, loud machinery, and shouting. The louder the sound, the more zombies it will attract from a larger radius. It is important for survivors to be mindful of their surroundings and limit any unnecessary noise.

Strategies: One strategy for minimizing noise pollution is using suppressors on firearms or opting for quieter weapons such as crossbows or melee weapons. Additionally, loud machinery like generators should only be used when absolutely necessary and with caution.

Distraction tactics can also be effective in drawing zombies away from an intended path. This can include using fireworks or other noisemakers in a different direction to divert their attention. Survivors may also use recordings of human voices or animal cries as decoys.

In summary, understanding the attraction of zombies to sound is crucial in navigating the wasteland safely and effectively. By minimizing noise pollution and utilizing distractions, survivors can decrease their chances of encountering large groups of zombies and increase their chances of survival.

2.3 Movement Patterns

Surviving in a world overrun by zombies requires a thorough understanding of their movement patterns. This chapter will outline the different ways in which zombies move and how to navigate these movements safely.

2.3.1 Urban Environments

Zombies tend to congregate in areas of high population density, such as abandoned cities and towns. They are attracted to these areas due to the presence of potential food sources (i.e. living humans). In urban environments, zombies tend to follow established pathways such as roads, sidewalks, and alleyways. This makes it easier for survivors to predict their movements and plan escape routes accordingly.

However, there are some risks associated with navigating through urban environments. Zombies can easily become stuck or bottlenecked in narrow spaces, creating large groups that are difficult to avoid or escape from. Survivors must also be cautious when entering buildings as they may encounter hidden pockets of zombies inside.

2.3.2 Rural Environments

Zombies in rural environments roam more freely. They are attracted to sources of food and water such as farms, livestock, and bodies of water. Due to the lack of established pathways and fewer population centers, it is more challenging to predict their movements in rural areas.

Strategy: To effectively navigate both urban and rural environments, survivors must study the local geography and understand potential hotspots for zombie activity. Avoiding high-risk areas, such as hospitals or shopping centers where large numbers of people may have been infected, can greatly increase their chances of survival.

Additionally, survivors should plan their routes carefully and always remain vigilant for potential threats. It is important to remember that zombies are always on the lookout for food sources and can quickly switch directions if they detect human presence.

In summary, understanding the movement patterns of zombies in different environments is essential for survival.

2.4 Feeding Frenzy

The most dangerous time for survivors is when they are detected by the undead. When a zombie first detects a human brain, a feeding frenzy occurs. And it is important to understand how to avoid becoming their next meal.

2.4.1 Detection

Zombies have an acute sense of smell and can detect the scent of living humans from a considerable distance. When they do, they enter a state of frenzy, becoming more aggressive and relentless in their pursuit.

Survivors must be aware of the signs that may attract zombies, such as loud noises or cooking smells. They should also be cautious when approaching potential sources of food, such as grocery stores or farms, as these areas may already be swarming with hungry zombies.

2.4.2 Avoiding Detection

To avoid being detected by zombies in a feeding frenzy, survivors must take precautionary measures. These include minimizing noise levels, avoiding strong scents like perfumes or cooking oils, and using cover to conceal movement.

Survivors should also use tools such as binoculars or drones to scout out potential threats before approaching an area. This will allow them to plan their movements accordingly and avoid being caught off guard by a large group of hungry zombies.

2.4.3 Escape and Evasion

If somehow a survivor does find themselves in the middle of a feeding frenzy, it is crucial to remain calm and not draw attention to themselves. Moving slowly and quietly can help to fly under the radar of frenzied zombies.

If escape is not possible, survivors can use distraction techniques such as throwing objects or creating loud noises in another direction to divert the attention of zombies away from them.

Survivors should also always have an escape plan in mind when entering any potentially dangerous area. It is important to be aware of surroundings and potential exit points constantly.

2.4.4 Conclusion

In conclusion, understanding how zombie detection works and taking preventative measures can greatly increase the chances of survival during a feeding frenzy. By remaining vigilant and having an escape plan, survivors can avoid becoming a part of the undead's next meal.

2.5 Identifying Wasteland Danger Zones

There are specific locations that pose a higher level of risk and require careful navigation to ensure safety. In this section, we will cover some of the most frequently encountered hazardous zones for survivors and provide strategies for successfully navigating them.

2.5.1 Urban Centers

Urban centers, such as cities or towns, are often hotspots for zombie activity because of the remnants of human civilization and the potential resources they offer. These areas are typically filled with abandoned buildings and narrow streets, creating opportunities for ambushes by zombies or hostile survivors.

Strategy: To navigate urban centers safely, survivors should move swiftly and quietly. Utilizing rooftops and alleyways can provide a stealthier approach to travel. It is essential to remain alert at all times and be on the lookout for potential threats lurking around every corner.

2.5.2 Highways and Roads

Highways and roads may seem like convenient routes for travel, but they also pose significant risks in a post-apocalyptic world. These areas are often filled with abandoned vehicles that can provide cover for zombies or bandits. The open terrain also makes it easier for zombies to spot survivors from a distance.

Strategy: Survivors should avoid traveling on highways and roads whenever possible. If travel is necessary, it is crucial to stay alert for potential threats along the way. Keeping a safe distance from abandoned vehicles can help reduce the risk of ambushes.

2.5.3 Rural Areas

Rural areas may seem safer than urban centers, but they still pose their own set of dangers in a post-apocalyptic world. These areas are often isolated and lack infrastructure, making it challenging to find resources or seek help if needed.

Strategy: When navigating rural areas, survivors should stick to main roads when possible and avoid venturing too far off into the wilderness. It is also important to be cautious when approaching farms or other potential sources of food as they may already be overrun by zombies.

2.5.4 Waterways

Waterways are often overlooked as a means of travel during a zombie apocalypse, but they can provide a way to move quickly and efficiently across long distances.

2.5.5 Hospitals and Morgues

Survivors may be tempted to search hospitals and morgues for valuable medical supplies, but these locations also pose significant risks. These facilities are likely to be abandoned, but they may still have reanimated corpses roaming the halls.

Strategy: Approaching hospitals and morgues should be done with extreme caution. Survivors should prioritize stealth and evasion over confrontation in these areas.

2.5.6 Military Installations

Characteristics: Fortified structures, potential for hidden dangers such as booby traps and hostile survivors. Military installations may offer valuable resources and equipment but are also likely to be heavily guarded and booby-trapped.

Strategy: Exercise extreme caution when approaching military installations, maintain a low profile to avoid detection, and be prepared to defend yourself if necessary.

2.5.7 Industrial Complexes

Characteristics: Abandoned factories, warehouses, and storage facilities. Industrial complexes may contain valuable resources and equipment, but also pose numerous hazards such as unstable structures and industrial machinery.

Strategy: Proceed with caution, be mindful of potential hazards such as chemical spills and machinery malfunctions and prioritize safety above all else.

2.5.8 Natural Hazards

Characteristics: Treacherous terrain, harsh weather conditions, and wildlife. Natural hazards such as rugged terrain, extreme temperatures, and dangerous wildlife can pose significant challenges to survivors.

Strategy: Plan your routes carefully, anticipate potential hazards, and be prepared to adapt to changing environmental conditions. Carry essential survival gear such as food, water, and shelter to mitigate the risks posed by natural hazards.

2.6 Other Wasteland Threats

While zombies pose the most widespread and persistent threat in the post-apocalyptic landscape, they are not the only dangers you may encounter. This section provides an overview of some additional perilous elements found in the wasteland.

2.6.1 Mutants

The nuclear fallout and environmental contamination have given rise to grotesquely mutated life forms: animals and even humans warped into unstable, highly aggressive abominations. While the degree of mutation varies, all should be considered extremely hazardous and unpredictable. Proper protective gear is essential when contact is unavoidable.

2.6.2 Raiders and Wasteland Warlords

In the absence of laws and civilization, bands of raiders, gangs and de-facto warlords have risen up to control precious resources and territory through violence and intimidation. Many are well-armed and willing to attack any outsiders encroaching on their domains. Understanding their tribal cultures and areas of influence is key to avoiding confrontations.

2.6.3 Other Organizations

Not all factions in the wasteland are overtly hostile. Remaining corporations, fringe groups, and even reborn societal movements may still be operating. However, their motivations and allegiances can be difficult to ascertain. Extreme caution is advised until their true intents and values are known.

2.6.4 Defended Communities

Pockets of survivors have banded together to eke out a new existence behind formidable defensive perimeters. While some may welcome outsiders, others may perceive any newcomer as a threat to their fragile way of life.

Approaching defended communities should only be done after extensive reconnaissance.

2.6.5 Armed Nomads

With no place to call home, these wandering survivor clans roam the wasteland, fighting over scant resources. Some groups are aggressive scavengers, while others are nomadic traders. Either way, they should not be underestimated as their combat skills and resourcefulness have kept them alive in the most desolate environments.

2.6.6 Non-human Threats

The wasteland environment has produced horrific new threats beyond the undead legions. From mutated animals to technological horrors, the arduous path to survival is littered with perils challenging the very limits of human understanding and endurance. Thorough study and preparation are vital to prevailing against these uniquely daunting wasteland dangers.

Mutated and Deranged Animals: The same contamination that spawned human mutations has also warped the animal kingdom. From snarling, radiation-crazed wolves and bears to insects growing to terrifying sizes, seemingly no species was spared from the ravages of the apocalypse. Exercise extreme caution around any animals exhibiting unnatural aggression, physical deformities, or abnormal sizes.

Unnatural Creatures: While their origins are uncertain, reports persist of utterly alien monstrosities now roaming the wastes. Whether spawned by toxic waste, volcanic phenomena, or forces beyond our comprehension, these abominations often display incredible sizes, grotesque anatomies, and violent predatory instincts. If encountered, evasion should be the priority unless combat is absolutely unavoidable.

Machine Scourges: Not all threats take a biological form. Automated robotic security drones, military weapons systems, and even re-animated machinery now hunt across certain zones of the wasteland, operating on remnant programming or damaged logic circuits. With no way to reason with these mechanical scourges, the only solution is to outwit, outmaneuver, or totally disable them through applied force.

While the zombie hordes remain the most widespread menace, these other wasteland elements each pose their own unique brands of danger.

Scavenging Essentials

In the harsh reality of the post-apocalyptic world, mastering the art of scavenging is essential for survival. This chapter will delve into the fundamental techniques, tools, and safety precautions necessary for successful scavenging missions in the wasteland.

3.1 Introduction to Scavenging

Scavenging, or the act of searching for and collecting usable materials or resources, has become a crucial part of survival in the post-apocalyptic world. With limited access to traditional means of acquiring food, water, shelter, and other essential items, scavenging has become a necessary skill for those trying to survive in this harsh new reality.

But scavenging is not just about randomly searching through debris and rubble; it requires strategy, knowledge, and proper equipment. In this chapter, we will discuss the fundamentals of scavenging and how to develop this critical survival skill.

3.2 The Purpose of Scavenging

The primary purpose of scavenging is to acquire resources that are necessary for survival. This includes food, water, medicine, weapons, ammunition, shelter materials, and any other useful items that can help you stay alive in the wasteland.

Scavenging also serves as a means of replenishing supplies and equipment that may have been lost or depleted during previous encounters with danger or other survivors. It is a continuous process that must be carried out regularly in order to sustain oneself in the long run.

3.3 The Basics of Scavenging

Before setting out on a scavenging mission, it's important to understand some basic principles that can help increase your chances of success. We use the acronym PUB, as in a PUB crawl. PUB however is no drinking game. It stands for Plan ahead, Use Caution, and Be Observant:

Plan ahead: Before venturing out into unknown territory for scavenging purposes, make sure you have a clear plan in mind. This includes identifying potential locations where valuable resources may be found and estimating how much time you will need to scavenge without risking exposure or running into danger safely.

Use Caution: Scavengers must always be cautious because the wasteland is filled with various hazards, such as radiation, traps, and hostile survivors. Therefore, it's crucial to take certain safety precautions before and during any scavenging mission.

Be Observant: When scouring an area for supplies, it's essential to pay attention to details. Look for signs of recent human activity or other potential dangers that may exist in the surrounding environment.

3.3.1 Essential Supplies for Scavenging

When heading out into the wasteland, it's crucial to be prepared with the right gear. The harsh and unpredictable conditions of the post-apocalyptic world require careful planning and strategic packing. In this chapter, we will discuss some essential supplies that every scavenger should have before embarking on a mission.

Food and Water: The most basic and essential supplies for any scavenger are food and water. Make sure to pack non-perishable items such as canned goods, protein bars, and dried foods that won't spoil easily. It's also important to have a supply of clean drinking water or a filtration system to purify any water sources you may come across.

Medical Supplies: Injuries and illnesses are inevitable in the wasteland, so it's crucial to have a well-stocked first aid kit with you at all times. This should include bandages, antiseptic wipes, pain relief medication, antibiotics, and any other necessary medications for potential health issues.

Tools: Having the right tools can make all the difference when scavenging. A multi-tool is a versatile item that can serve multiple functions such as cutting through wire or opening cans. A flashlight is also essential for navigating dark areas or searching through debris. Additionally, a crowbar can be useful for accessing locked or barricaded areas.

Protection: The wasteland is filled with various hazards that can pose a threat to your health and safety. Therefore, wearing appropriate clothing and gear is essential for protection against these dangers. This includes sturdy boots, protective eyewear, a gas mask for potential chemical hazards, and appropriate clothing layers depending on weather conditions.

3.3.2 Wasteland Buddies

In the harsh reality of the post-apocalyptic world, forming bonds and alliances can mean the difference between life and death. While survival instincts may tempt you to go it alone, having a trustworthy partner or "Wasteland Buddy" by your side can significantly increase your chances of success during scavenging missions.

Choosing a Wasteland Buddy is not a decision to be taken lightly. This person will be your constant companion, watching your back and sharing the burdens of survival. Ideally, your Wasteland Buddy should possess complementary skills to your own, allowing you to cover each other's weaknesses and approach challenges from different perspectives.

When selecting a Wasteland Buddy, look for individuals who demonstrate loyalty, level-headedness, and a strong moral compass. In a world where betrayal and selfishness can be commonplace, having a partner you can trust implicitly is invaluable.

Furthermore, it is crucial to establish clear communication and decision-making protocols with your Wasteland Buddy. Determine how you will resolve conflicts, divide responsibilities, and maintain situational awareness during scavenging missions. Practicing these protocols through simulations and drills will help solidify your partnership and ensure a seamless collaboration in the field.

Remember, your Wasteland Buddy is not just a partner in survival; they are a comrade-in-arms, a confidant, and a source of strength in the face of adversity. Cherish this bond, for it may be the key to enduring the harshest conditions and emerging victorious in the unforgiving wasteland.

3.4 Overall Mission Planning

Before embarking on any scavenging operation, conducting thorough map and intelligence-based reconnaissance and establishing a robust security setup is essential. This proactive approach ensures that your team is well-informed, prepared, and protected against potential threats lurking in the wasteland.

3.4.1 Pre-mission Reconnaissance and Planning

Before engaging in any scavenging activities, conducting a thorough top-level reconnaissance of the area and planning for the operation is vital. This allows you to gather intelligence on potential threats and assess the availability of resources.

Gather Intelligence: Gather as much information about the area as possible. This can include studying maps, talking to locals, or conducting aerial surveys if available.

Identify Potential Hazards: Look for potential hazards, such as hostile groups, natural obstacles, or dangerous structures that may pose a threat during scavenging.

Locate Points of Interest: Identify any points of interest that may contain valuable resources, such as abandoned buildings or warehouses.

Observe Enemy Activity: If hostile groups are in the area, observe their movements and routines to determine the best time to scavenge without being detected.

For more detailed information on this stage, see Section 4. Pre-operation Scouting and Planning.

3.4.2 Designate Operational Roles

Once you have gathered enough information about the area and identified potential threats, assigning roles within the Scavenging Operation is essential.

Security Team vs. Scavenging Team: The leader must divide the group into security and scavenging teams, each with specific roles and responsibilities. The size and composition of these teams depend on the operation's needs.

Wasteland Buddies: Wasteland buddies should not be split into different teams, if it is avoidable.

Meet Sierra's Crew

Throughout this survival manual, you'll see examples and case studies from real-life missions carried out by an experienced team of survivors known as Sierra's Crew. Led by the strategic Sierra and her second-in-command Casey, this group has endured more than its fair share of harrowing encounters with the undead . . . and the living.

Get acquainted with the core members that make up this resilient, battle-tested unit:

Sierra (Scavenge Leader) - The hardened overall leader and decision-maker. Sierra's calm mind and unwavering pragmatism have seen her people through many seemingly impossible scenarios. Her previous life as a humanitarian aid worker has uniquely prepared her to remain compassionate even when making the toughest of calls.

Casey (Assistant Scavenge Leader) - Utterly loyal and Sierra's right hand, Casey is a brilliant logistician capable of making the supplies and resources they scavenge go further than seems possible. His former career as a school counselor helps him foster discipline and mediate group tensions when morale runs low.

3.4.3 Security Team Formation

The Security Team, in a scavenging operation, is responsible for reconnaissance and security operations on the objective and en route to it. They will ensure that all zombies are (1) identified and appropriately eliminated (whether by destruction or by avoidance) prior to reaching the objective, (2) danger areas are cleared and secured before crossing them, and (3) any enemies or zombies are kept from entering the objective once scavenging operations begin. The security team may comprise the following roles:

Lookout Scouts: These team members should be stationed at strategic points overlooking the scavenging area to provide early warning of approaching threats.

Perimeter Guards: These team members should patrol the perimeter and look for suspicious activity or potential security breaches.

Sniper Support: If you have access to sniper support, they should be positioned at vantage points with clear sightlines of the scavenging area to provide cover and protection for your team.

Security Team members may be required to perform multiple roles, as teams are not usually large enough to have specialists in each of these areas, and operations are too fluid to be rigid. Therefore, Security Team members must be flexible, and be skilled in all different areas. Flexibility in adapting to operational needs is crucial.

Security Team:
Sam (Leader) - This former military officer brings an intensity of focus to security operations. His somber dedication to keeping the team safe at all costs means he constantly critiques and drills them on their tactics and procedures.

Riley - The team's stealthy pathfinder and scout, Riley's patient observation skills and quiet strength have saved lives more times than can be counted. Her pre-apocalypse work as a nature photographer fostered her attunement to the outdoors.

Alex - Carefree and fearless before the end, Alex was a thrill-seeker who loved pushing personal limits. Now his unerring marksmanship and steady nerves in the face of undead threats are invaluable assets as the squad's counter sniper.

Parker - Loyal to a fault, Parker will unleash unrelenting fury to protect any member of Sierra's family. Previously a nightclub bouncer, his imposing size and expertise in close-quarters combat have become essential for high-risk missions.

Dakota - Though seemingly quiet, Dakota more than compensates with her intellect, technical wizardry, and skill at surveillance/counter-scouting. A former IT analyst, her comms and cyber abilities give the crew an edge over threats.

3.4.4 Scavenging Team Formation

The Scavenging Team, in a scavenging operation, enters the objective, collects resources, and safely returns them to the designated safe zone. This team should be comprised of individuals with unique skills and abilities to collect resources and respond to unexpected situations. The scavenging team may include the following roles:

Fighters: The fighter breaches doors and clears rooms and other environments so that the other team members may scavenge. Fighters should be well-versed in weapons and experts in hand-to-hand combat with zombies and enemy survivors.

Gatherers: These individuals should be physically fit to carry heavy objects. They should also be good at spotting things and searching for things on the objective. They will collect and transport resources back to the safe zone.

Medic: In case of injuries or medical emergencies, it is crucial to have a member trained in first aid and basic medical care.

Mechanic: A mechanic can be invaluable in a scavenging operation, as they can identify useful items that can be repurposed or used for repairs.

The number of individuals needed for each role may vary depending on the size and complexity of the operation. Still, the group must ensure that all necessary skills are covered. In case of an emergency, some members may need to take on multiple roles, so cross-training is also vital.

Scavenging Team:
Hayden (Leader) - With an indomitable spirit and unwavering moral compass, Hayden's ability to make the tough calls while still lifting spirits is invaluable to Sierra. A motivational speaker before the fall, those skills translate perfectly now.

Emerson - Sierra's resident medic and voice of compassion. Emerson's empathy and level head keep the team grounded and offer comfort in their darkest hours. He was an ER nurse who committed to "first, do no harm."

Finley - An indispensable team member, Finley's incredible wilderness knowledge means he can forage food or lead the crew through any terrain. A former park ranger, Finley remains a welcoming, patient mentor to all.

Sutton - Seemingly born to defy the laws of physics and engineering, Sutton is Sierra's brilliant hands-on builder, mechanic and improviser. No piece of equipment or material is too damaged for this former construction worker to repurpose.

River - With almost preternatural urban movement abilities, River is the point scout who can infiltrate anywhere undetected. Formerly working high-risk security details, her skills lets her case sites and identify weaknesses the undead or hostile groups miss.

So be on the lookout for these capable, lively characters as their missions illustrate key survival principles covered in this manual. Their actions amid the zombie wasteland, and the meaningful personalities and backstories driving them, will make for memorable lessons you won't soon forget.

3.5 Operational Techniques

3.5.1 Establishing Security Measures on the Objective

Before any scavenging begins, it is necessary to set up defensive positions and lookout posts around the scavenging area.

Defensive Positions: Set up barricades and barriers around your base camp to prevent unauthorized access from hostile groups or potential looters.

Lookout Posts: These are stationed at strategic points to provide early warning, utilize concealment, and maintain 360-degree surveillance.

Sniper Positions: Snipers should be positioned to provide the most effective over watch of as much of the scavenging operation as possible.

3.5.1.1 Security Team Techniques

The Security Team plays a critical role in ensuring the safety and success of any scavenging operation. Effective security techniques and coordination among team members are essential for mitigating threats and protecting the scavenging team. Here are some key techniques for various security roles:

Lookout Scouts:

(1) Establish strategic observation points with clear lines of sight.
(2) Utilize terrain, vegetation, and camouflage for concealment.
(3) Maintain 360-degree surveillance, scanning for any signs of movement or threats.
(4) Quickly and accurately relay information on potential threats or hostile activity.
(5) Rotate positions and take breaks to maintain vigilance and alertness.

Perimeter Guards:

(1) Set up a clearly defined perimeter around the scavenging area, focusing on likely avenues of approach.
(2) Establish multiple layers of security, incorporating natural obstacles and fortifications.

(3) Patrol assigned sectors, maintaining a vigilant watch for breaches or intrusions.
(4) Employ the use of tripwires, early warning devices, and other detection methods, if expedient.
(5) Coordinate with lookout scouts and other teams for a cohesive security posture.

Sniper Support:
(1) Identify and occupy elevated positions or vantage points with clear lines of fire.
(2) Maintain strict noise and light discipline to avoid compromising positions.
(3) Accurately identify and prioritize targets, engaging only with authorization.
(4) Provide overwatch and suppressive fire support during engagements.
(5) Coordinate with other security elements to ensure seamless operations.

Engagement and Response:
(1) Maintain readiness and situational awareness at all times.
(2) Quickly and accurately assess threats, determining the appropriate response.
(3) Employ appropriate rules of engagement and escalation of force procedures.
(4) Coordinate with other security elements for a unified response.
(5) Maintain clear communication channels for reporting and requesting support.

Leadership and Coordination:
(1) Establish a clear chain of command and communication protocols.
(2) Develop contingency plans and rehearse various scenarios.

(3) Maintain overall situational awareness, receiving updates from all security elements.
(4) Make timely and informed decisions, adapting plans as situations evolve.
(5) Ensure the seamless rotation and relief of personnel to maintain operational effectiveness.

Effective security requires constant vigilance, attention to detail, and seamless coordination among all team members. By employing these techniques and fostering a culture of professionalism and discipline, the security team can effectively mitigate threats and ensure the success of scavenging operations in the unforgiving wasteland.

See Section 6.7 for strategies on adapting to changing conditions and maintaining situational awareness.

3.5.2 Scavenging the Objective:

Coordination and Communication: The security and scavenging teams should maintain constant communication to ensure effective coordination and response to threats.

Resource Prioritization: Focus on gathering essential items first, such as food, water, and medical supplies, while the security team maintains a vigilant watch for potential dangers.

Stealth and Evasion: Move quietly and stealthily to avoid attracting unwanted attention. Use cover and concealment to remain undetected by zombies or potential threats.

Systematic Search: Conduct a thorough sweep of the area, starting from the outskirts and working your way inward. Check every nook and cranny for hidden caches or valuable resources.

3.5.2.1 Scavenging Techniques

Scavenging requires a methodical approach to maximize efficiency and safety. Here are some techniques and considerations for key roles during scavenging operations:

Gatherers:

(1) Conduct systematic searches, moving methodically through each area and leaving no stone unturned.
(2) Check every nook, cranny, cabinet, and container for hidden or overlooked items.
(3) Prioritize essential resources like food, water, medicine, and ammunition.
(4) Use checklists or memory aids to ensure nothing is missed.
(5) Pack recovered items carefully using durable bags or containers to avoid damage.
(6) Consider weight distribution and mobility when collecting larger/heavier objects.

Fighters:

(1) Maintain a protective pivot, constantly scanning for threats as gatherers search.
(2) Clear paths, stairwells, and entrances to new areas before allowing gatherers to enter.
(3) Identify and dispose of potential hazards like traps or weakened structures.
(4) Establish rally points and fallback positions in case of enemy encounter.

(5) Utilize movement techniques like bounding overwatch to cover gatherers.

Medics:

(1) Keep medical supplies organized and easily accessible in case of injury.

(2) Triage and stabilize casualties, providing lifesaving care as needed.

(3) Ensure adherence to proper hygiene and sanitation protocols.

(4) Monitor team for signs of fatigue, dehydration, or other medical issues.

(5) Inventory and restock depleted medical supplies when possible.

Mechanics:

(1) Carefully inspect any recovered items/equipment for potential repurposing.

(2) Break down larger objects if transportable components can be used for repairs.

(3) Identify sources of raw materials like metals, wires, or chemicals.

(4) Improvise tools, weapons or fortifications from scavenged goods if needed.

(5) Maintain detailed logs of all items recovered and their potential uses.

Communications:

(1) Establish communications schedule and protocols like radio checks.

(2) Monitor all channels for updates on operations or potential threats.

(3) Quickly relay any situational updates between teams.

(4) Encode/encrypt any sensitive communications to prevent monitoring.

(5) Maintain backup communications methods in case of equipment failure.

Scavenging Process:

(1) Team leader briefs all members on specific objectives and areas to cover.

(2) Fighters take lead, clearing paths and establishing protective overwatch.

(3) Gatherers follow, thoroughly searching each area for resources.
(4) Other specialists like medics/mechanics follow, assisting as needed.
(5) Maintain communications discipline, relaying updates and locations.
(6) Package/consolidate resources carefully as areas are cleared.
(7) Backtrack and conduct thorough re-sweeps before moving to new areas.
(8) Rotate roles and responsibilities as needed to prevent combat fatigue.

By mastering these scavenging techniques and maximizing each role's expertise, teams can operate effectively to locate and secure valuable resources while mitigating risks during hazardous operations.

3.5.3 Travel to and from the Objective

Before the Scavenging Group reaches the objective, they may be required to traverse long distances through zombie or enemy survivor-infested areas. This travel must be conducted in an efficient and secure manner, avoiding detection if at all possible.

Command and Control

The first step in any successful scavenging operation is to establish a strong command structure. A designated leader should be responsible for making critical decisions and giving orders to the team. This leader should have sound judgment and be able to adapt quickly to changing situations.

It is also essential to establish communication protocols within the group. Radios or other forms of communication should be used to keep the team connected and informed at all times. In case of separation, pre-determined rally points should be established for regrouping.

Security Operations Around Dangerous Areas

As the Scavenging Group moves towards their objective, they must always be aware of potential threats from zombies or enemy survivors. It is vital to maintain situational awareness and conduct regular security checks on surrounding areas. Before crossing any danger area, security should be established. The level and depth of security is dependent on the operational need for speed and appetite for risk.

The group can use cover and concealment techniques while traveling through dangerous areas. These include staying low, moving quietly, and using natural barriers for protection.

If possible, routes should be pre-scouted before the actual operation begins to identify potential hazards or chokepoints that could slow down progress or expose the group to unnecessary danger. At a very minimum, a map reconnaissance should be conducted and a security plan developed for each identified danger area.

Movement and Formation Design

To adapt to terrain and operational needs, it is crucial to have a well-designed movement plan before starting any scavenging operation. The following are some important considerations:

Terrain: Scavengers must consider the terrain they will face during their travel towards their objective, as this will greatly affect their speed and mobility. For example, traversing rocky or hilly terrain will require more time than flat terrain.

Operational Needs: Depending on the type of resources being collected, the Scavenging Group's movement and formation design may vary. The Operation Leader should be flexible in their approach to travel.

Size of the team: The larger the team, the more important it is to manage the method of travel. Larger teams tend to attract more attention and be more difficult to control. Smaller teams are more agile and stealthy but are not able to carry as many scavenged resources or respond to ambushes and enemies with as much firepower.

The Objective Rally Point: After establishing communication protocols and preparing for security operations, the Scavenging Group should designate an Objective Rally Point (ORP). This is a pre-determined location where the group will regroup before moving on to the objective.

The ORP should be strategically chosen based on proximity to the objective and terrain considerations. It should not be within sight or hearing of the objective, but close enough for the group to conduct its operation efficiently and effectively.

Once the ORP is designated, the Scavenging Group should conduct a Leaders Reconnaissance of the objective. The Leader's Reconnaissance includes scouting the area for potential threats, obstacles, and any valuable resources that may need extra time or resources to collect.

After conducting a thorough reconnaissance, the group leader should discuss their findings with both the security and scavenging team leaders. This will ensure that all members are aware of potential dangers and have a clear understanding of their role in securing resources.

Security Plan: A comprehensive security plan must be developed at this stage to protect the Scavenging Group during their operation. This plan should consider potential threats from zombies or other survivors, as well as any natural hazards in the area.

The security plan should include specific roles and responsibilities for each member of the Security Team. This may include designated positions for lookout or perimeter defense, as well as procedures for reacting to enemy attacks or other unexpected situations.

Scavenge Plan: In addition to a security plan, a detailed scavenging plan must also be developed at the ORP. This plan identifies specific resources that need to be collected and their locations. It also outlines how these resources will be transported back to base camp.

The scavenging plan may involve dividing the Scavenging Team into smaller teams with assigned tasks such as gathering food, water, medical supplies, tools, or weapons. The amount of time spent on collecting resources should also be considered in this plan.

Contingency Plan: In any operation, it is important to have a contingency plan in case things do not go as initially planned. This is especially crucial in a post-apocalyptic world where resources and situations can quickly change.

The Scavenging Group should have a contingency plan in place before beginning their operation. This plan should address potential risks and alternative courses of action in case of unexpected events or challenges.

Survivor's Mindset

Traveling the wasteland is fraught with dangers, from zombie encounters to hostile survivors. Always have contingencies in place, and keep a proper mindset to minimize risks:

Situational Awareness: Remain vigilant at all times, scanning your surroundings for potential threats or hazards.

Avoidance Tactics: Whenever possible, choose routes that minimize exposure to danger zones and potential threats.

Escape Routes: Always have an escape plan in place in case you encounter danger and a well-rehearsed routine for disengagement with zombies and other enemies. Identify nearby exits or safe zones where you can retreat to safety if necessary.

3.6 Gear and Equipment

Proper gear and equipment are vital for survival in the harsh, unforgiving world of the post-apocalypse. Whether venturing out on scavenging missions or providing security for your team's operations, having the right tools and supplies can mean the difference between life and death.

This section covers the essential loadouts and gear recommended for both security team members and scavengers. From tactical vests and protective equipment to versatile multi-tools and supplies, each item has been carefully selected to maximize your chances of survival in even the most hostile environments.

Attention to detail is critical when gearing up. The equipment you choose to carry must not only be durable and functional, but easily accessible when needed. Proper packing and carrying techniques will allow you to quickly retrieve items without fumbling.

Maintaining and caring for your gear is just as important as selecting it. Regular inspections, cleaning, and preventative maintenance will ensure your equipment remains mission-ready at all times.

In the wasteland, your gear is your lifeline. Master its use and upkeep, for it may ultimately determine whether you survive the hazards or become another tragic casualty. Gear up, stay vigilant, and prepare to confront the dangers head-on.

3.6.1 Security Team Member Loadout

In a world where danger and violence are a constant threat, it is essential for security team members to be equipped with the right tools and gear to protect themselves and others. This chapter will cover the necessary items that should be included in a security team member's loadout.

On Person:

Combat Knife: A combat knife is a necessary tool for self-defense and close-quarters combat. It can also be used for various tasks like cutting through ropes or opening packages.

Sidearm with Extra Ammunition: A reliable handgun is an essential weapon for security team members. It should be carried on the person at all times, preferably in a holster attached to a tactical vest or belt. It's crucial to have extra ammunition readily available in case of extended engagements.

Tactical Vest: A tactical vest provides protection from gunfire and allows for quick access to essential items. Look for one with pouches specifically designed for ammunition, first aid supplies, and other necessary tools.

In Pack:

Additional Ammunition: Carrying extra ammunition in your pack ensures that you can replenish your supply if needed during an engagement.

Water Canteen: Staying hydrated is crucial, especially when actively engaged in security operations. Carry a durable water canteen and refill it whenever possible.

Energy Bars: Energy bars provide quick energy boosts when time does not allow for regular meals.

First Aid Kit: As mentioned earlier, injuries are common in dangerous environments, so having a well-stocked first aid kit is essential.

Binoculars: Binoculars can help identify potential threats from a safe distance and provide valuable information about the surrounding area.

Radio Communication Device: Staying connected with your team members is vital during security operations, especially if you need backup or assistance in an emergency situation.

3.6.2 Other Considerations:

Besides these basic items, there are some other things to consider when putting together a security team member's loadout.

Protective Gear: In addition to a tactical vest, security team members may also need other protective gear, such as helmets, knee and elbow pads, and ballistic goggles.

Comfortable Clothing: Choose clothing that is comfortable and allows for easy movement. Avoid loose-fitting clothes that can get caught on objects or restrict movement.

Good Boots: A durable pair of boots is essential for traversing rough terrain and providing support during long patrols.

Utility Belt: Additionally, there's a sturdy utility belt with carabiners and loops to attach tools like a multi-tool kit and a flashlight, ensuring readiness for any situation that may arise during scavenging missions.

3.6.3 Scavenging Team Member Loadout:

Scavenging is an essential task in any survival situation. Finding and gathering necessary resources such as food, water, and medical supplies can mean the difference between life and death. Scavenging team members should be equipped with specific items to help them carry out their duties effectively. This chapter will cover the necessary items that should be included in a scavenging team member's loadout.

On Person:

Multi-Tool: A multi-tool is a versatile tool that can come in handy for various tasks, such as cutting wires or opening cans.

Flashlight: A reliable flashlight is a must-have for any scavenging mission, as it may involve searching through dark and confined spaces.

Crowbar: A crowbar is a useful tool for prying open doors or containers. It can also be used for self-defense if needed.

Water Bottle: Staying hydrated is crucial during any physical activity, so carrying a water bottle is essential.

Respirator Mask: Hazardous materials or chemicals may be present in an urban environment, threatening your health. Having a respirator mask on hand can protect you from these dangers.

In Pack:

Non-Perishable Food Items: Scavenging often involves traveling long distances and expending energy, so carrying non-perishable food items like energy bars or dried fruits can provide quick sustenance when no other food sources are available.

Water Purification Tablets: If you come across water sources during your scavenging mission, having water purification tablets on hand allows you to safely consume the water without worrying about contamination.

Medical Supplies: Injuries are common when scavenging through potentially dangerous environments, so carrying basic medical supplies like bandages and antiseptics is essential.

Small Pry Bar: In addition to the crowbar securely fastened to the belt for easy access, a compact pry bar nestled in the side pocket of the pack can prove invaluable.

The Pack Itself: The pack itself should not be just a simple backpack but a tactical one, equipped with various compartments and pouches for organizing scavenged items efficiently.

Bags: Among these compartments are zippered bags of different sizes, perfect for storing anything from small trinkets to valuable finds.

Utility Belt: Same as above.

3.6.4 Other Useful Items

In addition to the essentials mentioned above, there are other useful items that can make your scavenging missions more successful.

Navigation Tools: It's important to have a way to navigate through the wasteland, especially if you're exploring unfamiliar territory. This could include a map of the area or a GPS device.

Communication Devices: In case of emergencies or if you're scavenging in a group, it's essential to have a way to communicate with others. This could be a two-way radio or a satellite phone.

Protective Gear: As mentioned earlier, protection is crucial in the wasteland. In addition to basic protective clothing and gear, consider adding items like knee and elbow pads for extra protection while crawling through debris.

Lockpicking Tools: Many valuable supplies may be locked away in abandoned buildings or vehicles, so having lockpicking tools can come in handy.

Rope and Grappling Hook: These tools can help you access higher areas or escape dangerous situations.

Duct Tape: This versatile tool has countless uses, from repairing equipment and clothing to creating makeshift shelters.

Personal Hygiene Supplies: Staying clean and healthy is important in the wasteland where germs and infections are prevalent. Pack items like hand sanitizer, wet wipes, and toilet paper for hygiene purposes.

3.7 Navigation and Mapping

Effective navigation is crucial for successful scavenging missions in the wasteland. Without a reliable map and sense, you risk getting lost or stumbling into dangerous areas. Here are some tips for navigating and mapping your way through the post-apocalyptic world.

3.7.1 Map Creation

Before heading out on your first scavenging mission, it's important to create a map of your local area. This map will serve as a reference point for future missions and help you navigate through the wasteland more efficiently.

To create a map, start by marking your current location as the center point. Then, use landmarks such as buildings, roads, and bodies of water to plot out the surrounding area. You can also use a compass and protractor for more accurate measurements and directions.

Next, mark locations of interest on your map, such as potential resource sites (abandoned buildings, farms, etc.), danger zones (infected areas, hostile territories), and safe havens (outposts, fortified camps). Having these marked on your map can save you time and effort during future missions.

Lastly, make sure to update your map regularly with any changes or new discoveries. This will ensure that you have an accurate representation of your local area at all times.

3.7.2 Route Planning

Once you have a basic map of your local area, you can start planning scavenging routes based on your objectives.

Consider factors such as terrain (avoid hazardous areas like swamps or steep cliffs), potential threats (hostile groups or infected creatures), and resource availability (areas with high concentration of resources).

If possible, try to plan multiple routes to reach your destination in case one becomes blocked or unsafe during your journey.

It's also important to keep track of where you've already scavenged in order to avoid revisiting the same locations multiple times.

3.8 Training Exercises

In order to survive in the wasteland, it's important to constantly improve your scavenging skills through training exercises. These exercises will not only help you hone your skills but also allow you to test and improve your gear and equipment.

3.8.1 Simulated Scavenging Missions and Rehearsals

One of the best ways to practice your scavenging skills is by participating in simulated scavenging missions. These missions are designed to mimic real-world scenarios and test your abilities in a controlled environment.

To start, gather a group of fellow survivors and choose a location for the simulation, such as an abandoned building or an overgrown forest. Assign roles within the group, such as leader, navigator, and scavenger.

The objective of the mission is to successfully scavenge for resources while avoiding potential dangers such as traps, infected creatures, and hostile groups. The leader should assign tasks to each member based on their strengths and weaknesses.

During the simulation, make note of any challenges or difficulties encountered and discuss ways to overcome them as a group. This will help you better prepare for similar situations in the future.

3.8.2 Navigation Challenges

Navigation is a crucial skill for successful scavenging missions. One way to improve this skill is by setting up navigation challenges in different environments. Some examples include:

Night navigation: Use only a map and compass (or other navigational tools) to navigate through an area at night.

Urban navigation: Navigate through a city using buildings and streets as landmarks.

Water navigation: Use a boat or raft to navigate through bodies of water.

These challenges will help you become more comfortable with navigating through different environments without relying on technology or visual aids.

3.8.3 Physical Training

Scavenging requires physical stamina and strength to traverse rough terrain and carry heavy loads. Incorporate physical training into your routine to build the physical conditioning necessary to survive in the harsh environment of the wasteland and the rigors of scavenging and other operations.

3.9 Conclusion

As you embark on your scavenging mission, remember that preparation and vigilance are key to survival. By mastering the essentials of scavenging, you can navigate the wasteland with confidence and secure the resources needed to thrive in the post-apocalyptic world.

Pre-operation Scouting and Planning

The success of a scavenging mission often hinges on thorough reconnaissance and operational planning. This chapter delves into the essential techniques and considerations for scouting and planning, equipping you with the knowledge and skills necessary to navigate the wasteland with precision and purpose.

4.1 Introduction to Pre-operation Scouting and Planning

Scavenging isn't just about blindly searching for resources; it's about gathering intelligence, analyzing risks, and strategically mapping your path. Learn why scouting and planning are essential components of successful scavenging missions.

4.2 Pre-mission Reconnaissance During Scavenger Missions

A thorough reconnaissance is vital before venturing into the dangerous terrain of the zombie-infested world. This section outlines the crucial steps to take before and during a scavenging mission to ensure the safety and success of your team.

Conducting extensive pre-mission reconnaissance is crucial before setting out on a scavenging mission. This involves gathering information, assessing risks, and formulating a plan of action to maximize the chances of success and minimize the potential dangers.

Analyzing Terrain and Obstacles

Topography Assessment: Study the area's maps to understand the terrain, including elevation changes, water bodies, and natural shelters, ensuring a smoother navigation process.

Scouting Routes: Identify potential routes to and from the scavenging site, considering factors such as visibility, cover, and potential hazards like zombie concentrations or collapsed structures, to chart a safe course.

Obstacle Identification: Look for obstacles such as rubble, barricades, or impassable terrain that may impede your progress. Develop strategies to navigate or circumvent these obstacles safely to ensure efficient movement.

Gathering Intelligence

Local Knowledge: Tap into any remaining local communities or survivors for information about the area, including potential dangers, resources, and hidden caches, providing invaluable insights into the environment.

Scavenger Reports: Gather intel from previous scavenging missions or survivor groups to learn about the area's current state, including any recent zombie activity or changes in the environment. This will aid in informed decision-making.

Remote Surveillance: Use drones, surveillance cameras, or telescopic optics to scout the area from a safe distance and gather valuable information without risking direct exposure, ensuring reconnaissance without compromising safety.

Planning for Contingencies

Emergency Extraction Points: Identify multiple emergency extraction points along your planned route in case you encounter unforeseen dangers or need to evacuate quickly, ensuring a swift exit in case of emergencies.

Backup Plans: Develop alternative plans for accessing the scavenging site or retrieving essential resources in case your primary plan encounters unexpected obstacles or threats, ensuring adaptability in dynamic situations.

Emergency Supplies: Pack emergency supplies, including first aid kits, communication devices, and extra ammunition, to ensure your team is prepared to handle any unexpected situations that may arise, prioritizing safety and readiness for unforeseen circumstances.

Assessing Security and Threats

Threat Assessment: Evaluate potential security risks, including the presence of zombies, hostile survivors, or environmental hazards, and develop strategies to mitigate these threats, prioritizing the safety of the team.

Security Measures: Implement security measures such as perimeter patrols, lookout posts, and secure communication protocols to minimize the risk of ambush or detection during the mission, ensuring operational security.

Concealment and Camouflage: Utilize natural cover, camouflage, and stealth techniques to avoid detection by zombies or other hostile entities while conducting reconnaissance or scavenging activities, maximizing stealth and minimizing risks during operations.

Quarryville: Sierra's reconnaissance plan sets the foundation

Weeks of careful recon and planning had identified an abandoned medical supply depot that could replenish their dwindling stocks. But first, Sierra had to ensure the operation's security.

Following the pre-mission process to the letter, she ordered Casey to oversee establishing a secured Objective Rally Point in the nearby woods, just out of sight from their target - the quarry facility.

With the ORP being hardened by Sam's security teams, Sierra and Casey slipped away to conduct the critical Leader's Reconnaissance. Utilizing forward scout Riley's detailed reports, they meticulously surveyed the quarry's exterior from every vantage point.

Sierra took note of the various access vectors that would need interlocking fields of fire covered to prevent enemy ingress. She also identified a potential

centralized location for Hayden's scavenging crew to focus their search efforts around.

Returning to the ORP, Sierra gathered all elements and relayed her security plan based on the recon results . . .

4.3 Mapping Out Scavenging Routes

Creating a Scavenging Map: Landmarks, Hazards, and Alternate Routes.

After completing reconnaissance and gathering intel, it's time to create a detailed map of your scavenging route. Here are the key steps to follow:

4.3.1 Landmark Identification

Marking landmarks on your map is crucial for efficient navigation and resource acquisition. Consider including the following landmarks:

Stores: Marking stores, supermarkets, pharmacies, and other potential sources of food, water, medical supplies, or equipment provides crucial waypoints for resource acquisition.

Shelters: Identifying shelters, safe houses, bunkers, or buildings with fortified structures in case of emergencies or inclement weather ensures the team has refuge options along the route.

Water Sources: Mapping out nearby lakes, rivers, streams, or wells for potential refill points ensures the team remains hydrated during the mission.

Fuel Stations: Noting gas stations or depots where vehicles can be refueled is essential for ensuring mobility and operational readiness during the mission.

Communication Towers: Marking communication towers or high ground with clear visibility for potential radio transmission or signaling purposes enhances the team's ability to maintain communication and coordinate with other groups.

Medical Facilities: Identifying hospitals, clinics, or medical centers allows the team to access medical supplies, facilities, or expertise in case of injuries or emergencies during the mission.

Weapon Depots: Mapping out armories, military bases, or areas known for weapons storage can provide the team with additional firepower or equipment resources if needed.

Community Centers: Noting community centers, town halls, or gathering places where survivors may congregate can facilitate interactions with local communities and gathering of valuable intelligence.

Lookout Points: Identifying elevated positions or natural lookout points with good visibility of the surrounding area allows the team to maintain surveillance and monitor for potential threats or opportunities.

Vehicle Repair Shops: Marking auto repair garages or workshops where vehicles can be serviced or repaired ensures the team can address mechanical issues and maintain vehicle functionality during the mission.

Power Stations: Noting power stations, substations, or electrical infrastructure can provide insights into potential energy resources or vulnerabilities in the area.

Military Installations: Identifying military bases, outposts, or checkpoints may provide the team with access to additional supplies, equipment, or strategic advantages if properly approached and negotiated.

Historical Landmarks: Marking significant landmarks, monuments, or cultural sites can serve as reference points and contribute to the team's understanding of the area's history and geography.

Trails: Identifying established trails, footpaths, or hiking routes can provide efficient routes for travel, especially in rugged terrain or areas with dense vegetation. Trails may offer advantages such as easier navigation, reduced risk of encountering hazards, and access to scenic or hidden locations.

Roads: Mapping out roads, highways, streets, and thoroughfares is essential for planning vehicular travel routes. Roads often provide the fastest and most direct paths between locations, facilitating efficient movement of vehicles and equipment. However, roads may also pose risks such as congestion, vehicle blockages, or ambush points, so alternative routes should be considered.

Bridges: Noting the locations of bridges, overpasses, or river crossings is crucial for crossing bodies of water or impassable terrain. Bridges provide strategic chokepoints and critical infrastructure for maintaining mobility and access to resources. However, bridges may also be vulnerable to damage, sabotage, or collapse, so their condition should be carefully assessed before use. Additionally, alternative crossing points such as fords or makeshift crossings should be identified as backup options in case bridges are unavailable or compromised.

4.3.2 Hazards Assessment

Hazards can pose serious risks during scavenging missions. Be sure to identify and mark potential hazards on your map to avoid them during your expedition. These may include:

Zombie-Infested Areas: Marking areas with high zombie activity allows the team to plan routes that minimize the risk of confrontation with the undead.

Collapsing Buildings: Identifying unstable structures that could potentially collapse during your mission helps the team steer clear of dangerous areas.

Natural Disasters: Noting areas prone to floods, earthquakes, or other natural disasters ensures the team avoids hazardous environments that could jeopardize their safety.

Radiated Water: Identifying sources of radiated water, such as contaminated rivers, lakes, or reservoirs, is crucial for avoiding exposure to harmful radiation. These areas may be marked as high-risk zones on the map, and alternative water sources should be sought to prevent contamination of supplies and minimize health risks to the team.

Structures or Plant Life: Noting structures such as collapsed buildings, unstable infrastructure, or overgrown vegetation can pose hazards such as falling debris, entanglement, or concealment of threats. These areas should be approached with caution, and potential hazards should be marked on the map to ensure safe navigation.

Dead Areas with Persistent Chemical Weapons Residue: Identifying areas contaminated with persistent chemical weapon residue, toxins, or hazardous substances is essential for avoiding exposure and minimizing health risks. These dead zones may have lingering chemical agents or environmental hazards that pose immediate danger to the team. Avoidance is key, and protective equipment may be necessary if travel through these areas is unavoidable.

Mutant Plants, Animals, or Fauna: Noting locations where mutated or genetically altered plants, animals, or fauna are known to inhabit can pose unique hazards such as aggressive behavior, toxic secretions, or unpredictable behavior. These areas should be approached with extreme caution, and encounters with mutant creatures should be avoided if possible.

Wasteland Raiders and Outposts: Marking locations of known wasteland raiders, bandit camps, or hostile outposts is essential for avoiding confrontations and navigating safely through contested territory. These areas may be patrolled by armed groups intent on looting or attacking travelers, so vigilance and stealth are critical when passing through these regions.

Minefields: Identifying areas where minefields or improvised explosive devices (IEDs) are present is crucial for avoiding accidental detonation or injury. These hazardous areas may be marked on the map as restricted zones, and caution should be exercised when navigating through unfamiliar terrain to avoid setting off explosives.

Other Hazardous Areas: Noting locations of other potential hazards such as collapsed tunnels, unstable cliffsides, or hazardous waste dumps ensures the team is aware of potential dangers in the area. These areas should be avoided or approached with extreme caution to minimize risks to the team's safety and success of the mission.

4.3.3 Alternative Routes

It's important to have backup plans in case your original route becomes impassable because of unforeseen circumstances. Consider mapping out alternative routes for different scenarios, such as:

Heavy Zombie Activity: Planning a route away from high concentrations of zombies provides a fallback option if the team encounters unexpected hordes.

Blocked Roads: Creating alternate paths in case roads become blocked by debris or obstacles ensures the team can navigate around obstructions without compromising the mission.

Weather Conditions: Considering alternate routes if severe weather affects your primary path allows the team to adapt to changing environmental conditions and maintain progress towards their objectives.

Terrain Variation: Identifying alternative routes that offer different terrain characteristics can provide strategic advantages such as better cover, reduced exposure to hazards, or opportunities for stealthy movement. For example, choosing routes through dense forests, rocky terrain, or urban areas may offer different levels of concealment and protection.

Elevation Changes: Mapping out alternative routes that involve changes in elevation, such as hills, ridges, or valleys, can provide tactical advantages such as improved vantage points, natural barriers, or opportunities for ambush or evasion. Consideration should be given to the impact of elevation changes on visibility, fatigue, and overall mission objectives.

Vegetation Cover: Noting alternative routes that offer dense vegetation cover, such as forests, jungles, or brushy terrain, can provide concealment and camouflage opportunities for the team. These routes may offer protection from aerial surveillance, observation by hostile forces, or adverse weather conditions.

Water Crossings: Identifying alternative routes that involve crossing bodies of water, such as rivers, streams, or marshes, provides options for bypassing obstacles or avoiding congested areas. Consideration should be given to the availability of suitable crossing points, potential hazards such as currents or waterborne threats, and the impact on travel time and resources.

Urban Areas: Mapping out alternative routes that traverse urban or built-up areas offers opportunities for shelter, resupply, and navigation landmarks. Urban routes may involve navigating streets, alleyways, or building interiors, presenting challenges such as restricted mobility, potential ambush points, or encounters with hostile forces or civilians.

Rural Areas: Identifying alternative routes that pass through rural or agricultural areas offers opportunities for open terrain, reduced population density, and access to natural resources such as food, water, and shelter. Rural routes may involve navigating fields, pastures, or farmsteads, presenting challenges such as exposure to environmental hazards, encounters with wildlife, or limited access to infrastructure.

Infrastructure: Noting alternative routes that utilize existing infrastructure, such as roads, bridges, or tunnels, provides options for rapid movement, access to communication networks, and navigation landmarks. Consideration should be given to the condition of infrastructure, potential hazards such as collapse or sabotage, and the presence of hostile forces or checkpoints.

Stealth and Concealment: Identifying alternative routes that prioritize stealth and concealment, such as avoiding main roads, populated areas, or known enemy positions, can provide opportunities for surprise, evasion, or infiltration. These routes may involve off-road navigation, use of natural terrain features, or nighttime travel to minimize detection and maximize operational security.

4.3.4 Return Routes

As part of the planning process, it's essential to establish return routes to safely navigate back to the base or safe zone after completing the scavenging mission. These routes should consider factors such as changes in terrain, potential hazards, and the weight carried from the scavenging mission. It's crucial to note that a scavenger team should never take the same way out as they took in to avoid ambush, trackers, zombies, or mutants that have picked up their trail.

Weight Consideration: When planning return routes, the team must consider the additional weight they'll be carrying from the scavenging mission. Heavy loads can impact mobility, endurance, and overall mission success. Routes should prioritize efficiency and minimize unnecessary detours or obstacles to accommodate the team's increased burden.

Use of Vehicles or Horses: If available, vehicles or horses can significantly expedite the return journey, especially when transporting heavy or bulky items acquired during the scavenging mission. Return routes should take advantage of roads, trails, or open terrain suitable for vehicular or equestrian travel, optimizing speed and efficiency while minimizing exposure to hazards.

Vehicle Exfiltration: When planning return routes using vehicles, the team must consider factors such as fuel consumption, vehicle maintenance, and potential mechanical failures. Routes should prioritize access to fueling stations, repair facilities, or alternative transportation options to ensure the team can reach their destination safely and without delay.

Terrain Adaptation: Return routes should take into account any changes in terrain or environmental conditions encountered during the scavenging mission. Team members should be prepared to adapt to challenges such as inclement weather, natural obstacles, or hostile encounters, adjusting their route as needed to maintain progress towards their objective.

Avoiding Detection: To minimize the risk of detection by hostile forces, zombies, or mutants, return routes should vary from the initial approach route. Team members should use different paths, alternative landmarks, or diversionary tactics to throw off pursuit, evade potential threats, and maintain operational security throughout the return journey.

Stealth and Vigilance: Return routes should prioritize stealth and vigilance to avoid attracting unwanted attention or encountering hostile forces along the way. Team members should remain alert to their surroundings, maintain situational awareness, and employ stealthy movement techniques to minimize the risk of detection and maximize their chances of reaching safety unharmed.

By carefully planning return routes and considering factors such as weight carried, mode of transportation, and operational security, the scavenger team can safely navigate back to base after completing their mission, ensuring the successful acquisition of valuable resources while minimizing risks to personnel and equipment.

4.4 Identifying Key Locations

Knowing where to scavenge is just as important as knowing how to scavenge. Identify and prioritize key locations based on factors such as:

4.4.1 Resource Abundance

Targeting areas with high concentrations of valuable resources, such as:

Food: Prioritize locations with abundant food sources, including supermarkets, grocery stores, farms, and urban gardens. Consider seasonal availability and perishability when planning scavenging missions.

Water: Identify sources of clean water, such as rivers, lakes, reservoirs, or water treatment facilities. Ensure access to potable water for hydration, cooking, and sanitation purposes.

Medical Supplies: Locate pharmacies, hospitals, clinics, or medical facilities where essential medical supplies, medications, and equipment may be found. Consider the urgency and importance of medical resources for treating injuries or illnesses.

Tools and Equipment: Seek out hardware stores, construction sites, or industrial facilities where tools, equipment, and materials for repairs, construction, or improvised weaponry may be obtained. Prioritize items that enhance the team's survival and operational capabilities.

4.4.2 Security Risks

Assessing the level of danger posed by various threats in different locations, including:

Zombie Activity: Avoid areas with high concentrations of zombies or signs of recent undead activity. Prioritize locations with minimal zombie presence to minimize the risk of confrontation or ambush during scavenging missions.

Hostile Survivors: Beware of hostile survivors, bandits, or raiders who may pose a threat to the scavenger team. Avoid areas known for criminal activity, violence, or territorial disputes, and exercise caution when interacting with unknown individuals or groups.

Environmental Hazards: Consider environmental factors such as natural disasters, hazardous terrain, or extreme weather conditions that may pose risks to the team's safety and well-being. Plan scavenging missions accordingly to mitigate the impact of environmental hazards on operational effectiveness.

Radiation Zones: Steer clear of areas contaminated by radiation or other hazardous materials, such as nuclear fallout zones or industrial sites with radioactive waste. Minimize exposure to radiation to prevent radiation sickness and long-term health effects.

4.4.3 Accessibility

Considering the ease of access to potential scavenging sites and the feasibility of navigating the terrain, including:

Terrain Analysis: Assess the topography, geography, and infrastructure of the area to determine the best routes for reaching scavenging locations. Prioritize sites that are easily accessible by foot, vehicle, or other means of transportation, while avoiding obstacles such as impassable terrain, collapsed structures, or natural barriers.

Distance and Travel Time: Evaluate the distance and travel time required to reach each scavenging location, considering factors such as route complexity, mode of transportation, and potential delays. Prioritize sites that are within a reasonable distance and can be reached safely within the allotted time frame for the mission.

Stealth and Discretion: Consider the importance of maintaining stealth and discretion during scavenging missions to avoid detection by hostile forces or unwanted attention from zombies or mutants. Choose routes and locations that offer cover, concealment, and strategic advantages for covert operations while minimizing the risk of exposure or engagement with adversaries.

By carefully identifying and prioritizing key scavenging locations based on resource abundance, security risks, and accessibility factors, the scavenger team can maximize their chances of success while minimizing risks to personnel and resources during missions in the Wasteland.

4.5 Leader's Pre-Mission Inspection

Before any high-risk scavenging mission, it is essential for the team leader to conduct a comprehensive pre-mission inspection. This systematic process ensures that all personnel, equipment, and provisions are fully prepared and mission-ready. Drawing from time-honored Army tactics, the pre-mission inspection follows the principle of "Inspect what you Expect."

4.5.1 Personnel Inspection

The leader begins by inspecting each team member individually, ensuring they are physically and mentally fit for the rigors of the upcoming operation:

Physical Readiness: Check for any injuries, fatigue, or illness that may impact performance.

Mental Readiness: Assess alertness, focus, and the ability to follow orders precisely

Equipment Checks: Inspect individual gear like weapons, ammunition, optics, and communications.

Uniform and Protection: Verify proper dress, camouflage, helmets, and body armor if applicable.

4.5.2 Equipment Inspection

Next, the leader methodically inspects all team equipment and provisions for the mission:

Vehicles/Transportation: Conduct preventative maintenance, check fuel, make any repairs.

Heavy Weapons/Explosive Breaching Tools: Ensure proper operation, handling, and security.

Rations and Water: Verify adequate field rations and potable water for the operation's duration.

Specialty Tools/Gear: Test functionality of metalworking tools, breaching gear, comms equipment.

Medical Supplies: Inventory and prepare for potential trauma, sickness, or exposure incidents.

4.5.3 Mission Brief Back

As part of the inspection, the leader requires key personnel to brief back critical aspects of the mission:

Mission Objectives: Team leaders restate the goals, tasking, and intent of the operation

Specific Responsibilities: Individuals recount their assigned roles, duties, and areas of responsibility

Contingency Plans: Members recount actions in case of enemy contact, casualties, or other emergencies

Operational Timeline: Restate the timeline, routes, rally points, and other key temporal events

Rules of Engagement: Review guidelines for use of force, deadlines, weapons status at each stage

4.5.4 Remediation and Re-Inspection

If any deficiencies are identified during the inspection, the leader takes corrective actions:

Refit/Resupply Equipment: Replace or refurbish any faulty gear before stepping off

Additional Training/Rehearsals: Conduct refresher instruction on any skills found lacking

Personnel Reassignments: Shift responsibilities or re-organize fireteams if required

Adjust Mission Timeline/Plan: Make any final updates to allow for remediation

Only once the leader is fully satisfied that every shortcoming has been identified and addressed is the team certified as prepared for the upcoming operation. This pre-mission inspection ensures professional standards and attention to detail, minimizing preventable failures once the mission is launched.

4.6 Training Exercises

Aligned with the core topic of scouting and planning, training exercises are pivotal in preparing scavenger teams for the challenges of the post-apocalyptic world. By focusing on scouting skills, planning methodologies, and operational readiness, these exercises ensure teams are equipped to navigate hazardous environments, gather vital intelligence, and execute successful missions.

Reconnaissance Drills: Devote significant attention to reconnaissance drills, emphasizing the gathering of actionable intelligence and meticulous terrain analysis. Practice techniques such as map reconnaissance, aerial observation, and ground surveillance to develop a comprehensive understanding of the operating environment.

Map Reading and Navigation: Enhance proficiency in map reading and navigation through immersive training scenarios. Emphasize the interpretation of topographic maps, route planning, and navigation techniques to foster spatial awareness and ensure accurate decision-making during missions.

Security Protocols and Procedures: Incorporate security protocols and procedures into training exercises to mitigate risks and maintain operational security. Conduct simulated scenarios involving perimeter defense, threat detection, and response tactics to instill a culture of vigilance and readiness within the team.

Scenario-Based Training: Utilize scenario-based training to simulate real-world missions and challenge teams to apply scouting and planning skills in dynamic situations. Incorporate elements of uncertainty, time pressure, and resource constraints to test adaptability, decision-making, and teamwork under stress.

Team Coordination and Communication: Foster effective team coordination and communication through collaborative training exercises. Practice leadership, delegation, and task allocation to ensure clear roles and responsibilities are established within the team. Encourage the use of standardized communication protocols and tactical signaling to enhance situational awareness and cohesion during missions.

Rehearsals and Repetition: Emphasize the importance of rehearsals and repetition to internalize procedures and develop muscle memory. Conduct regular rehearsals of mission plans, response protocols, and contingency procedures to ensure readiness and responsiveness in high-pressure situations.

Standard Operating Procedures (SOPs): Develop comprehensive SOPs to standardize practices, enhance efficiency, and promote consistency among team members. Document procedures for reconnaissance, planning, execution, and debriefing to ensure a common understanding of expectations and protocols across the team.

After-Action Reviews (AARs): Conduct thorough AARs following each training exercise to facilitate learning, identify areas for improvement, and refine tactics, techniques, and procedures. Encourage constructive feedback, self-reflection, and collaborative problem-solving to drive continuous improvement and readiness for future missions.

By integrating these elements into training exercises, scavenger teams can cultivate the scouting and planning skills necessary to navigate the post-apocalyptic landscape with precision, confidence, and effectiveness.

4.7 Conclusion

As you venture into the wasteland, remember that knowledge and preparation are your greatest weapons. By mastering the techniques of scouting and planning, you can navigate the dangers of the post-apocalyptic world with confidence and purpose, ensuring the success of your scavenging missions and the survival of your team.

Effective Scavenge Operations

5.1 Introduction to Effective Scavenging

In the chaos of the post-apocalyptic world, effective scavenging can mean the difference between life and death. We'll explore the fundamental principles and tactics that will enable you to scavenge efficiently and safely, ensuring the survival of yourself and your team.

5.2 Systematic Resource Identification

Before embarking on a scavenging mission, it's crucial to identify and prioritize the resources you need. We'll discuss techniques for systematically scanning your environment, categorizing resources based on their value and utility, and prioritizing acquisition based on immediate needs and long-term sustainability.

5.3 Efficient Search and Retrieval Methods

Scavenging is not just about finding resources; it's about retrieving them efficiently and safely. Learn how to organize search efforts, manage inventory, and transport recovered resources. We'll cover techniques for searching buildings, vehicles, and other structures, as well as methods for safely extracting and transporting valuable items.

5.4 The Scavenging Operation:

Scavenging operations are complex. They consist of multiple stages, all of which are required to maximize your chances of success. These are:

Reconnaissance: Survey the area for possible resources, dangers, and barriers. Set up a security boundary to keep threats from entering the area while Reconnaissance is underway. The goal of the Reconnaissance is to evaluate risks and opportunities on the target and decide if the potential gains of the scavenge operation outweigh the risk, and provide needed information to plan and execute the Scavenging Operation.

Security: Secure the scavenging area to minimize the risk of encountering threats during the operation. Set up perimeter defenses and lookout posts on all key avenues of approach to monitor for approaching threats.

Clearing the Area: Before beginning the search/scavenging process, clear the area of any immediate threats. Engage and eliminate any zombies or hostile survivors present in the area.

Scavenging Operation: Conduct the search/scavenging process to identify and collect valuable resources. Utilize the chosen scavenging strategy (e.g., block by block, room by room) to ensure thorough coverage of the area.

Exfiltration: Safely exit the scavenging area with acquired resources and return to a secure location—retreat from the scavenging area while maintaining security and vigilance for potential threats.

Leave No Sign or Trail: Cover your tracks to minimize the risk of detection by zombies or competing groups. Conceal any evidence of your presence in the area, such as footprints or discarded items.

5.4.1 Patrol to the Objective Rally point:

After completing the necessary planning and reconnaissance phases, it's time for the team to begin their approach to the objective rally point (ORP). This critical stage of the operation requires careful coordination, security measures, and implementing appropriate movement techniques.

5.4.1.1 Formation

One of the first decisions the team leader must make is the formation in which the team will move. The chosen formation should balance factors such as security, maneuverability, and control. Here are some common formation options and their considerations:

- **File Formation:** In this formation, team members move in a single line, one behind the other. This formation is suitable for narrow terrain or when stealth is a priority, as it minimizes the team's signature. However, it can be vulnerable to enfilade fire and limits situational awareness.

- **Staggered File Formation:** This formation is similar to the file formation but with team members staggered to either side, providing more security and situational awareness. It is versatile and can be adapted for various terrain conditions.

- **Wedge Formation:** In this formation, the team spreads out in a V-shape, with the point element leading the way. This formation offers good security and observation to the front and flanks and is suitable for more open terrain or when encountering potential threats.

- **Ad-hoc Formations:** Depending on the situation, the team leader may need to adapt and create custom formations to suit the terrain, threats, or mission requirements. This could involve variations of the standard formations or entirely new configurations.

When deciding on the appropriate formation, the team leader should consider factors such as the terrain, potential threat levels, visibility conditions, and the team's size and capabilities. Clear communication and adherence to established movement techniques and protocols are crucial during this phase to ensure a smooth and secure approach to the ORP.

5.4.1.2 En route Information Gathering:

During the journey to the scavenging site, the team engages in en route information gathering to gather valuable intelligence and insights that can inform their mission approach and decision-making process. Here's a sequential series of actions typically undertaken during this phase:

Engage with Locals: As the team travels through the area, the leader encourages interaction with any remaining local communities or survivors encountered along the way, provided these locals do not pose a threat to the Scavenging Operation or the team. Engaging with locals allows the team to gather firsthand accounts of recent events, potential dangers, and resources in the area.

Establish Trust: Building rapport and trust with locals is essential for obtaining accurate and reliable information. The leader and team members approach interactions with empathy, respect, and a willingness to listen, fostering open communication and cooperation. It is important to keep in mind, however, that this interaction is always done with sufficient security to ensure the safety of the Team as they work to establish trust. The Security Team should always provide overwatch and security on this interaction.

Verify Information: While gathering intelligence from locals, the team exercises critical thinking and discernment to assess the credibility of the information received. They cross-reference details with other sources and evaluate the consistency and reliability of the information before incorporating it into their decision-making process.

Observe Surroundings: As the team travels, they remain vigilant and observant of their surroundings, noting any signs of recent activity, potential threats, or valuable resources along the route. This situational awareness helps the team identify opportunities and threats in real-time, allowing for timely adjustments to the mission plan.

Document Findings: The leader ensures that any valuable information gathered during the journey is documented systematically, including details such as locations of potential resources, observations of enemy activity, or insights from local interactions. This documentation is a reference for future planning and informs the team's decision-making process.

Adapt Strategy: Based on the information gathered en route, the leader and team members adapt their strategy and approach to the mission as needed. They may revise route plans, adjust resource allocation, or modify tactics to account for new insights or changing circumstances encountered during the journey.

Maintain Communication: Throughout the en-route information-gathering process, the leader maintains open communication with team members, ensuring that everyone is informed of relevant developments and contributing insights as needed. Effective communication fosters teamwork and enables the team to respond quickly and decisively to emerging opportunities or threats.

By engaging in en-route information gathering, the team maximizes their situational awareness, enhances their understanding of the operating environment, and increases their ability to make informed decisions during the scavenging mission. This proactive approach to intelligence collection strengthens the team's effectiveness and resilience in the face of the challenges posed by the Wasteland environment.

5.4.1.3 Movement Techniques and Security Measures

As the team moves towards the Objective Rally Point (ORP), it is essential to maintain a high level of situational awareness and implement various security measures to mitigate potential threats. These measures include conducting listening halts, security halts, establishing rally points along the route, and having a clear plan for reacting to potential enemy contact.

Listening Halts: Listening halts are short, planned stops during movement where the team freezes in place and remains silent for a brief period. These halts serve two primary purposes:

1. Detect any potential threats in the area by listening for unusual sounds or movement.

2. Allow the team to regain situational awareness and ensure proper dispersal and formation integrity.

Listening halts should be conducted at irregular intervals and in concealed locations whenever possible.

Security Halts: Security halts are more extensive stops where the team takes up temporary defensive positions and conducts a thorough 360-degree scan of the surrounding area. These halts are typically initiated at terrain features that could potentially conceal enemy forces, such as intersections, hilltops, or tree lines.

During a security halt, the team leader may assign individual team members specific observation sectors, ensuring comprehensive coverage of the area. This measure helps identify potential threats early and allows for a timely reaction if necessary.

Reaction to Contact: In the event of unexpected enemy contact or hostile activity during movement, the team must have a well-rehearsed plan for reacting and seeking cover. This plan should include:
(1) Immediate suppression of the enemy force to prevent escalation.
(2) Rapid dispersal and occupation of covered and concealed positions.
(3) Establishing a base of fire to allow for maneuver or disengagement.
(4) Initiation of a casualty evacuation plan if necessary.

The team leader's guidance and coordination are crucial during these situations to ensure a cohesive and effective response.

Establishing Rally Points: To maintain operational cohesion and facilitate regrouping in case of separation or enemy contact, the team leader should identify and communicate rally points along the planned route to

the ORP. These rally points should:
(1) Be easily recognizable terrain features or landmarks.
(2) Provide adequate cover and concealment.
(3) Allow for multiple approach routes.
(4) Be known to all team members.

By implementing these security measures and having a clear plan for reacting to potential threats, the team can mitigate risks and increase their chances of reaching the Objective Rally Point safely and efficiently.

Danger Areas: During the movement to the ORP, the team may encounter areas that pose a higher risk or potential danger. These could include open areas with limited cover and concealment, potential ambush sites, or locations with known enemy activity. The team leader should identify these danger areas in advance and implement measures to mitigate the risks.

Possible measures for navigating danger areas include:
(1) Changing the movement formation to provide better security and observation.
(2) Increasing the use of bounding overwatch or other movement techniques.
(3) Employing additional security elements or overwatch positions.
(4) Adjusting the route to avoid the danger area if possible.

The team leader should also consider the potential need for actions on contact, such as breaking contact or engaging the enemy, depending on the specific. Danger areas should not be negotiated without proper security in place unless speed is essential for mission success. In such cases, the team leader should ensure measures are taken to reduce any potential risk associated with sacrificing security for speed.

By implementing these measures and referring to additional resources, the team can enhance its operational security and increase its chances of reaching the Objective Rally Point safely and efficiently while minimizing the risk of enemy contact or other potential threats.

5.4.2 Objective Rally Point

Once the objective rally point (ORP) is reached, the team leader assesses the situation and makes critical decisions before the rest of the team proceeds with the mission. Here's a sequential series of actions typically taken during this phase:

Establish Security: The team leader immediately establishes security at the ORP to protect the team from potential threats while conducting the reconnaissance. This ensures the team's safety and prevents any surprises from adversaries.

Survey Surroundings: The leader conducts a thorough visual and auditory survey of the immediate surroundings, noting any potential hazards, terrain features, or signs of enemy presence. This provides valuable information for planning the next steps of the mission.

Verify Objective Location: The leader confirms the location of the mission objective relative to the ORP, ensuring that the team is in the right position to execute the mission effectively. This helps prevent confusion and ensures alignment with the overall mission plan.

Assess Terrain: The leader analyzes the terrain surrounding the ORP, considering factors such as elevation, cover, and potential avenues of approach. Understanding the terrain is crucial for developing a sound plan of action and maximizing the team's effectiveness during the mission.

Conduct Leader's Reconnaissance: The next section addresses this function in detail.

5.4.2.1 Leader's Reconnaissance

Once the objective rally point (ORP) is secured and established, the critical next step is for the team leader to conduct a comprehensive reconnaissance of the area. This leader's reconnaissance allows for a thorough assessment of the situation, identification of potential threats or hazards, and the development of a detailed plan of action before committing the rest of the team to the mission.

The leader's reconnaissance is a methodical process that should cover several key aspects, including:
(1) Identifying potential rally points or fallback positions in case of enemy contact or other emergencies.
(2) Evaluating threats and developing contingency plans for various scenarios.
(3) Planning the movement and coordination of the team from the ORP to the objective, including assigning roles and responsibilities.

The information gathered during the leader's reconnaissance is crucial for making informed decisions and ensuring the safety and success of the overall operation.

Identify Rally Points: The leader identifies potential rally points and fallback positions within the vicinity of the ORP, providing the team with strategic locations to regroup or seek cover in case of enemy contact or other emergencies. This enhances the team's flexibility and resilience during the mission.

Evaluate Threats: The leader assesses potential threats in the area, including enemy forces, zombies, or environmental dangers. By identifying and prioritizing threats, the leader can develop effective risk mitigation strategies and ensure the safety of the team throughout the mission.

Plan Movement: Based on the information gathered during the reconnaissance, the leader develops a detailed plan for moving from the ORP to the mission objective. This includes determining the best route, assigning responsibilities to team members, and establishing communication protocols to maintain cohesion and situational awareness.

5.4.2.2 Rally Points and Fallback Positions

During the Leader's Reconnaissance, identifying potential rally points and fallback positions is crucial to ensure the team's safety and ability to regroup in case of unforeseen circumstances or enemy contact. These predetermined locations serve as critical contingency measures and play a vital role in maintaining operational flexibility and cohesion.

Rally Points: Rally points are designated areas where the team can reassemble or regroup in case they become separated or need to disengage from the objective area, or while conducting the patrol to the Objective Rally Point. Establishing rally points allows for a coordinated response and prevents team members from becoming isolated or lost.

When selecting rally points, the team leader should consider the following factors:

Proximity: Rally points should be located within a reasonable distance from the objective area, allowing for a swift and efficient regrouping process.

Concealment and Cover: Rally points should provide adequate concealment from enemy observation and cover from potential threats, ensuring the team's safety during the regrouping phase.

Accessibility: Rally points should be easily accessible from multiple directions, allowing team members to converge from various locations within the operational area.

Identifiable Terrain Features: Rally points should be located near distinct terrain features or landmarks, making them easily recognizable and reducing the risk of confusion or disorientation.

Fallback Positions: Fallback positions are predetermined defensive locations where the team can temporarily retreat or take cover in case of enemy contact or overwhelming threats. These positions provide a secure area for the team to regroup, receive medical attention, and plan their next course of action.

When identifying fallback positions, the team leader should consider the following factors:

Defensibility: Fallback positions should offer natural or man-made defensive advantages, such as elevated terrain, robust structures, or easily fortifiable positions.

Fields of Fire: Fallback positions should provide clear fields of fire, allowing the team to effectively engage threats from multiple directions.

Resupply and Extraction: Fallback positions should have access to potential resupply routes or extraction points, ensuring the team can receive reinforcements or evacuate if necessary.

Concealment and Cover: As with rally points, fallback positions should offer adequate concealment and cover to protect the team from enemy observation and fire.

By identifying and communicating rally points and fallback positions during the Leader's Reconnaissance, the team leader ensures that contingency plans are in place to maintain operational cohesion, facilitate regrouping, and mitigate risks in case of unforeseen circumstances or enemy contact.

5.4.2.3 Scavenge Plan Development

Resource Prioritization: The leader works with team specialists to identify and prioritize the resources needed during the scavenging mission. This prioritization is based on the team's immediate needs, long-term sustainability requirements, and the potential value or utility of the resources.

Task Organization: The leader organizes the scavenge and security teams into specialized elements or squads, assigning specific tasks and responsibilities to each member or sub-unit. This may include designating search teams, security details, medical personnel, and logistics support.

Search Methodology: Based on the information gathered during reconnaissance and the nature of the objective, the leader determines the most appropriate search methodology to be employed. This could involve strategies such as the Outside-in Method or Block-by-Block Method. Once the appropriate area Search Method is decided upon, the leader will need to decide whether Bottom-to-Top or Room-to-Room Search procedures will be necessary for each individual building.

Evacuation/Exfiltration Planning: The leader develops a comprehensive plan for evacuating or exfiltrating the team and any acquired resources from the objective area. This includes identifying primary and alternate routes, establishing rally points, and coordinating transportation or extraction methods if necessary.

Quarryville: ORP

. . . Dakota would monitor all communications from an overwatch position, providing top cover in the tree line. Riley and Alex would be deployed forward as scouts/snipers screening for any hostile movement attempting to approach the objective area. Parker, with his formidable skills in weapons and close-quarters combat, would anchor the main fortified position covering their rear exfiltration path out.

Quickly but methodically, Sam's security teams moved into their pre-planned support-by-fire positions ringing the quarry objective while Hayden's scavenging elements stood by to move on Sierra's initiation signal.

The quarry searched without incident for the first two hours as the scavengers followed their search methodology, locating and consolidating crates of invaluable drugs, equipment, and other vital medical supplies. That's when Parker's voice crackled across the radio net, "Contact front! Incoming hostile!"

5.4.3 Scavenging Strategies

The choice of Method can often be the deciding factor between success and failure. As the team leader, a myriad of factors accumulated during pre-mission reconnaissance, events on the patrol, and the Leader's Reconnaissance inform your decision on the Scavenging Method chosen. Drawing upon all information gathered about the environment, potential threats, and operational characteristics, you must weigh the advantages and disadvantages of each Method to determine the most suitable approach for the mission at hand. Your leadership, strategic thinking, and adaptability are paramount as you navigate the challenges of the wasteland and lead your team to survival amidst uncertainty and danger.

5.4.3.1 Outside-In Method

The Outside-In Method entails a perimeter assessment before moving inward, offering a cautious yet comprehensive approach to scavenging.

When to Use: This Method is best suited for situations where the perimeter of the scavenging area can be easily accessed and secured. It's ideal for teams looking to conduct a preliminary assessment of the area's overall viability before committing to a more thorough search.

Ideal Situations: The Outside-In Method is particularly effective in urban environments with clearly defined boundaries, such as fenced-off neighborhoods or industrial complexes. It can also be used in rural areas with natural barriers, such as forests or rivers, that allow for perimeter scanning.

Team Size Consideration: This Method is suitable for both small and large teams, as it primarily involves reconnaissance and perimeter security, which can be scaled based on team size.

Inherent Risks: The major risk associated with the Outside-In Method is limited visibility of interior spaces, which may result in missed opportunities or threats going unnoticed until the team moves inward.

Advantages:

(1) Allows for a comprehensive assessment of the area without immediate exposure to potential threats.

(2) Provides an opportunity to identify entry points and potential obstacles before committing to interior searches.

(3) Minimizes the risk of encountering immediate threats by maintaining a secure perimeter.

(4) Facilitates strategic decision-making by providing a broad overview of the scavenging area.

Disadvantages:

(1) Limited visibility of interior spaces may make it difficult to assess potential resources or threats within buildings or structures.

(2) Relies heavily on effective perimeter security measures to prevent threats from entering the area during reconnaissance.

(3) May delay the start of interior searches, potentially prolonging the overall scavenging operation.

(4) Requires careful coordination to ensure that reconnaissance efforts cover all potential entry points and perimeter vulnerabilities.

5.4.3.2 Block-by-Block Method

The Block-by-Block Method divides the scavenging area into manageable sections, ensuring methodical coverage and minimizing oversights.

The Block-by-Block Method involves dividing the scavenging area into smaller blocks and systematically searching each one before moving on to the next. This approach ensures thorough coverage and minimizes the risk of missing potential resources or threats.

Ideal Situations: The Block-by-Block Method is effective in urban environments with grid-like street layouts or multi-block structures, as well as in large-scale industrial complexes or warehouses with multiple compartments or storage areas.

Team Size Consideration: While this Method can be adapted to accommodate both small and large teams, larger teams may have an advantage in terms of manpower for simultaneous searches of multiple blocks.

Inherent Risks: The main risk associated with the Block-by-Block Method is its potential for time-consuming searches, which may increase exposure to threats if not properly coordinated and secured.

Advantages:

(1) Ensures thorough coverage of the scavenging area, minimizing the risk of overlooking valuable resources.

(2) Allows for a methodical and organized approach to scavenging, reducing the likelihood of missed opportunities or duplication of efforts.

(3) Facilitates efficient resource allocation by dividing the scavenging area into manageable sections for search and clearance.

(4) Provides a clear framework for task delegation and coordination within the team, enhancing overall effectiveness and efficiency.

Disadvantages:

(1) Can be time-consuming, especially in larger scavenging areas with extensive block layouts or multiple structures.

(2) May increase the risk of exposure to threats if not properly coordinated and secured, particularly if search efforts are spread thin or poorly synchro-

nized.

(3) Requires careful planning and coordination to ensure that each block is thoroughly searched and cleared before moving on to the next.

(4) May be less adaptable to dynamic or rapidly changing situations, as searches must proceed in a systematic and sequential manner.

Quarry: Withdrawal to the ORP

A horde of undead, likely alerted by the team's movement or street noise, came pouring hungrily across the quarry floor towards the scavenger's position. Sierra immediately initiated the contingency plan, ordering Hayden's team to withdraw back to the ORP.

Despite having transited carefully to avoid giving away their location, the scavenging crew was cut off by one scrambling group of zombies . . . then another . . . and another. Everywhere they turned, more undead blocked the path back to the ORP's protective cordon.

It was the defensive overwatch that saved them. Dakota's voice was a whirlwind of coordinates as she targeted the first groups of shamblers through her scope. Alex and Riley added their exact fire from the forward positions, temporarily disrupting and stalling the undead's inexorable approach.

Halfway back to the ORP, Hayden's team ran into one last winding trail of zombies blocking their retreat. But Parker's covered killzone simultaneously engaged with disciplined marksmanship and brutal firepower, ripping that final pocket of hostiles into shreds.

Battered but unbowed, the scavengers finally made it back past Parker's lines to the ORP, where Casey was readying their supplies for exfiltration . . .

5.4.4 Building Clearing Tactics

Often times when conducting the Scavenge Operation, regardless of what method chosen, the Scavenge team will be faced with clearing buildings in order to accomplish the mission objectives. The following procedures should be followed when faced with such obstacles.

5.4.4.1 Room-by-Room Procedures

When clearing individual rooms or compartments within a building, the Room-by-Room procedure should ensure a thorough and methodical search, minimizing the risk of overlooking hidden threats or valuable resources.

Procedure:

(1) Establish security outside the room, covering all potential entry/exit points.
(2) Assign roles (e.g., breach team, security team, search team, based on their roles and skills).
(3) Conduct a thorough visual and audio inspection of the room from the entry point.
(4) The breach team enters and clears any immediate threats if deemed clear.
(5) The security team follows, establishing overwatch positions within the room. If there are insufficient team members for both a security and breach

team, these team members will conduct both missions.

(6) The search team then enters and conducts a systematic search, following established patterns (e.g., pie-shaped, clockwise/counter-clockwise).

(7) Check all potential hiding spots, furniture, and compartments for resources or threats.

(8) Once the room is thoroughly searched, consolidate any resources found.

(9) Mark the room as cleared and secure the exit point.

(10) Repeat the procedure for each subsequent room or compartment.

Considerations:

(1) Maintain strict communication and control during room clearance.

(2) Be prepared to respond to potential threats or ambushes within confined spaces.

(3) Ensure proper lighting and visibility within each room.

(4) Have contingency plans for evacuation or breaking contact if necessary.

By following these building clearing procedures, scavenging teams can effectively and safely search multi-level structures or individual compartments, ensuring thorough coverage and minimizing the risk of overlooking valuable resources or potential threats.

5.4.4.2 Bottom-Up Procedures (Multi-level Buildings)

When clearing multi-level structures during scavenging operations, the Bottom-Up procedure should be employed to methodically and thoroughly search each floor from the bottom up. This approach ensures comprehensive coverage while minimizing the risk of overlooking valuable resources or hidden threats on higher levels.

Procedure:

(1) Establish security on the ground level, ensuring no immediate threats

are present.

(2) Assign team members to their roles (e.g., security, search, overwatch).

(3) Clear and secure the ground level using room-by-room techniques (see 5.4.4.1).

(4) Once the ground level is clear, establish a staging area for consolidating resources.

(5) Position security elements to cover stairwells and potential entry points to upper levels.

(6) Conduct a thorough search of the next level up, following room-by-room procedures.

(7) Repeat step 6 for each subsequent level, ensuring lower levels remain secured.

(8) As higher levels are cleared, reposition security elements to maintain overwatch.

(9) Continue the systematic search until all levels have been thoroughly cleared.

Considerations:

(1) Leave minimum security elements behind on cleared lower levels when possible to maintain integrity of secured areas.

(2) If stairwells can't be completely cleared, have contingencies for breaking contact back to lower levels.

(3) If faced with overwhelming resistance, upper-level teams should bound back to cleared lower levels.

(4) Maintain constant communication between teams on different levels.

(5) Be prepared to respond to potential threats from higher/unsecured levcls.

(6) Have contingency plans for evacuation or breaking contact if necessary.

5.5. Stealth and Evasion Tactics

In a world overrun by zombies and hostile survivors, stealth is your best friend. We'll explore techniques for moving quietly, using cover and concealment to avoid detection, and minimizing noise and visibility. Whether you're navigating through abandoned buildings or sneaking past zombie hordes, these tactics will help you stay hidden and out of harm's way.

5.5.1 Noise Discipline

Even the slightest sound can carry for miles, potentially giving away your position to undead hordes or hostile survivors. Maintaining strict noise discipline is therefore critical for any team conducting scavenging or reconnaissance operations.

Maintaining Silence: Team members must learn techniques for moving quietly, such as careful foot placement, avoiding loose debris, and controlling gear. Noise can compromise the element of surprise and alert threats to your presence.

Communication Methods: Visual signals or hand signs should be used to avoid making sounds that could be detected. If voice communications are required, they should be kept at a whisper.

Equipment Handling: Proper equipment handling is crucial. Items should be tightly secured to prevent rattling, and weapons should have any unnecessary accessories removed to reduce their noise signature.

5.5.2 Use of Terrain and Cover

While noise discipline helps keep you unheard, concealment and the proper use of terrain are vital for keeping your team unseen as well. The wasteland environment, whether urban or rural, offers ample opportunities for camouflage and using natural or man-made materials to mask your presence.

Identifying Concealment: Teams should look for natural terrain features like hills, trees, buildings, or manmade trench lines that can hide their presence and mask their movements from potential threats.

Natural Camouflage: In rural environments, disrupting your outline and matching the surrounding vegetation and ground patterns through camouflage netting or foliage can aid in concealment.

Urban Movement Techniques: In cities, teams should master the skill of using shadows, window indents, doorways, and any available hard cover to avoid detection while moving between positions.

5.5.3 Light Discipline

As if maintaining stealth during the day wasn't difficult enough, night operations introduce an entirely new set of challenges for avoiding detection. Even the faintest glow from a light source can instantly compromise your position when darkness falls.

Visible Light Procedures: At night, visible light sources must be tightly controlled. Flashlights should only be used briefly with lenses covered. Red lens filters reduce the ability of threats to detect the light source.

Night Vision Considerations: When using night vision devices, teams must mask any stray light emissions that could alert threats. Maintaining 360-degree security is critical, as threats may also have night vision capabilities.

5.5.4 Counter-Tracking

In addition to avoiding detection through stealth, teams must also implement counter-tracking measures to prevent threats from following their movements or determining where they originated from:

Use of Terrain Obstructions: Travel through areas with heavy brush, rocky terrain or urban rubble to disrupt and obscure tracks.

Deception Measures: Laying false trails, covering footprints, and doubling back can confuse threats trying to follow your path.

Limited Travel in Open Areas: Avoiding extended travel across unobstructed open ground where tracks may easily be visible.

5.6 Utilization of Tools and Equipment

The right tools can make all the difference during a scavenging mission. The Team Leader should determine what equipment is needed based on the Pre-mission Planning, and the Leader's Reconnaissance. The following are some examples of equipment to be considered based on the Scavenging Operation parameters:

Pry Bars, Bolt Cutters: These portable tools allow teams to force open locked doors, gates and remove chains/locks when stealth entry is not required. Various sizes are used based on the application.

Breaching Charges/Explosives: When rapid and explosive entry is needed into a hardened structure, frame charge explosives or other man-portable breaching tools may be used by trained personnel for forced entry.

Flashlights, Cameras: High powered tactical flashlights and cameras mounted on weapons allow teams to safely inspect and record the interiors of structures prior to entry. Thermal optics can detect heat signatures.

Entry Kits, Fiber Optics: Remote video scouts allow teams to inspect tight spaces and multi-level structures prior to personnel entering. Fiber optic cameras feed back real-time video for threat assessment.

Shovels, Pick Mattocks: Sturdy, multi-purpose digging tools are essential for excavating through rubble or potential buried caches.

Probing Rods: Long rigid rods inserted into the ground at intervals can detect subsurface obstructions or voids that may indicate buried resources.

Durable Packs/Bags: Built to withstand tough conditions, high-quality backpacks and duffel bags allow the safe transportation of acquired resources over long distances and varied terrain.

Carts/Sleds for Heavy Loads: For heavier or bulky resources, improvised carts, sledges or makeshift skids assist teams in transporting the loads more efficiently.

5.7 Resource Preservation and Management

In the unforgiving landscape of the post-apocalyptic wasteland, resources are finite and incredibly valuable. Scavenging is vital, but even more critical is making those hard-won supplies last. Effective preservation and management are key to long-term survival. This section covers essential techniques for:

Food Storage and Rationing

(1) Properly preserving perishable items through dehydration, curing, smoking

(2) Portion control and weight/nutrition balancing of rations

(3) Inventory management to rotate stocks and prevent spoilage

Water Acquisition and Recycling

(1) Locating and purifying freshwater sources

(2) Rainwater collection and distillation methods

(3) Greywater recycling systems for reusing non-potable supplies

Equipment Maintenance

(1) Cleaning, repair, and preventative upkeep

(2) Locating or improvising replacement parts and tools

(3) Maximizing operational lifespan through proper use and care

Repurposing and Recycling

(1) Breaking down scrap for raw materials

(2) Improvised crafting of gear, tools, and fortifications

(3) Environmentally sustainable practices

By implementing these preservation and management principles, you can ensure critical resources go further and increase your self-sufficiency. Careful husbandry, not just acquisition, may determine who outlasts the unforgiving wasteland.

5.8 Team Coordination and Communication

No one survives the apocalypse alone. Teamwork and cohesion are force multipliers that can mean the difference between life and death on scavenging operations. This section covers key principles for operating as a unified team, including:

Defined Roles and Responsibilities

(1) Clear leadership hierarchies and decision-making protocols

(2) Understanding every team member's specific assignments

(3) Coverage of essential tasks like security, search, medical, etc.

Situational Awareness and Operational Updates

(1) Maintaining a shared understanding of the environment

(2) Communicating updates on any tactical developments

(3) Building team reflexes through rehearsals and contingency drills

Communication Techniques and Protocols

(1) Hand/arm signals and coded messages to maintain stealth

(2) Backup communication plans and rallying procedures

(3) Strict radio discipline and authentication measures

Adaptability and Contingency Response

(1) Delegating new roles and responsibilities when required

(2) Coordinating actions in response to escalating threats

(3) Resolving inner-team conflicts with emotional intelligence

By mastering these coordination and communication skills, teams can operate as a highly cohesive and situationally aware force. This synchronization enhances survivability and the ability to capitalize on opportunities when they emerge amidst the chaos of the wastes.

5.9 Training Exercises and Simulation

Put your scavenging skills to the test with practical training exercises and simulations. We'll conduct role-playing scenarios to simulate real-world scavenging situations, allowing you to practice your skills and decision-making abilities in a controlled environment. These exercises will help you build confidence and preparedness for actual scavenging missions.

Radio Procedures: Standardized practices like use of pro-words, encrypted communications, radiotelephony procedures and breach load plans are critical for clear communications.

Visual Signals/Markers: Colored smoke, flares, glo-patches, and hand/arm signals provide backup communication methods when radio discipline is required.

Countersurveillance: Teams must take active measures like security patrolling and aerial surveillance to detect any potential threats watching or trailing their operations.

Managing Unit Signatures: Steps like camouflage, noise/light/litter discipline and minimizing any electronic emissions prevent potential threats from detecting your presence.

Contingency Reactions: Immediate action battle drills for scenarios like Zombie contact, breaking contact, vehicle ambushes, or med-evacs must be practiced extensively.

Team/Crew Level Drills: Mission specific collective tasks involving all members working in concert should undergo detailed rehearsals to improve coordination, confidence and reaction time.

5.10 Conclusion

As you continue your journey through the post-apocalyptic world, remember that effective scavenging is not just about finding resources—it's about surviving against all odds. By mastering the techniques and strategies outlined in this chapter, you can scavenge efficiently and safely, ensuring the survival of yourself and your team in the face of adversity.

Survival and Exfiltration to Base

Survival in the post-apocalyptic world demands more than just luck—it requires meticulous planning, resourcefulness, and adaptability. In this chapter, we will explore the essential survival strategies and techniques necessary for navigating the dangers of the wasteland and safely returning to base after a mission. From assessing survival needs to implementing security measures and coordinating exfiltration, this chapter equips you with the knowledge and skills needed to thrive in even the most challenging environments.

6.1 Introduction to Survival Strategies

Before venturing into the unknown, it is crucial to understand the importance of survival strategies. In the unforgiving landscape of the post-apocalyptic world, a well-crafted survival strategy can mean the difference between life and death. Effective survival planning ensures that your team is prepared to face any challenge, from securing essential resources to defending against potential threats.

At the core of any successful survival strategy lies the ability to identify and address basic needs. Food, water, shelter, and security form the foundational pillars upon which all other aspects of survival are built. By developing a comprehensive plan to meet these fundamental requirements, you can establish a solid foundation for resilience and success in the face of adversity.

Moreover, survival strategies encompass not only the physical aspects of sustaining life but also the mental and psychological fortitude required to persevere in the harshest of conditions. From fostering teamwork and effective communication to maintaining morale and adapting to changing circumstances, a well-rounded survival strategy addresses the multifaceted challenges of the wasteland.

6.2 Assessment of Survival Needs

Survival begins with a clear understanding of your most basic needs. Failing to accurately assess and prioritize these needs can quickly lead to disastrous consequences. In this section, we will delve into the process of evaluating and addressing the core survival requirements of food, water, shelter, and security.

6.2.1 Assessing Food and Water Needs

Ensuring a reliable source of sustenance is paramount in the wasteland. Determining your group's caloric requirements based on activity levels and environmental conditions is the first step in assessing food needs. Once you have established a baseline, you can begin identifying potential food sources in your immediate surroundings, such as edible plants, hunting opportunities, or scavenged non-perishable items.

Water, the lifeblood of survival, requires equal attention. Evaluate the availability of water sources in your area, taking into account factors such as proximity, purity, and potential contamination risks. Be prepared to implement purification methods, such as boiling, filtration, or the use of purification tablets, to ensure a safe and consistent supply of drinking water.

6.2.2 Evaluating Shelter Requirements

Shelter is a vital component of survival, providing protection from the elements, predators, and potential threats. When evaluating shelter requirements, consider the size of your group, the local climate, and the availability of materials for construction or fortification.

Assess the need for defensive capabilities within your shelter, factoring in the potential presence of hostile forces or dangerous wildlife in the area. Prioritize locations that offer natural barriers or strategic advantages, allowing for easier fortification and enhanced security.

6.2.3 Analyzing Security Threats

In the lawless expanse of the wasteland, security is a constant concern. Conduct a thorough threat assessment, identifying potential hostile forces, dangerous wildlife, or environmental hazards that could jeopardize your survival. Evaluate your vulnerabilities and exposure risks, considering factors such as visibility, access routes, and potential choke points.

Based on your analysis, determine the necessary measures for protection and concealment, including defensive structures, camouflage techniques, and early warning systems. Remember, vigilance and preparedness are key to mitigating security threats in the post-apocalyptic world.

6.3 Development of Survival Plans

Armed with a comprehensive understanding of your survival needs, the next step is to develop a cohesive plan that addresses each aspect, ensuring your team's resilience and long-term sustainability in the wasteland.

6.3.1 Establishing Clear Objectives and Priorities

Begin by defining your short-term and long-term survival goals. These objectives will serve as a guiding compass, helping you allocate resources effectively and make informed decisions throughout your journey.

Prioritize your critical needs, such as securing food, water, and shelter, over non-essential objectives. However, be mindful that priorities may shift as circumstances change, requiring adaptability and flexibility in your planning.

Align your objectives with the resources and capabilities available to your team, ensuring that your goals are realistic and achievable given your current situation.

6.3.2 Resource Allocation and Management

Conduct a thorough inventory of your available supplies, including food, water, medical resources, and equipment. Ration these resources judiciously, allocating them based on your prioritized needs and the urgency of each situation.

Plan for resource replenishment or identify alternative sources to ensure a sustainable supply chain. This may involve scavenging missions, establishing trade relationships with other survivor groups, or exploring renewable resource options such as gardening or water collection systems.

6.3.3 Contingency Planning

No survival plan is complete without contingencies for unforeseen circumstances. Identify potential risks and threats that could disrupt your primary objectives, such as natural disasters, supply shortages, or hostile encounters.

Develop backup plans for various scenarios, including alternative routes, fallback positions, and emergency protocols. Establish rally points and rendezvous locations in case your team becomes separated, ensuring a coordinated response and increasing the chances of reuniting safely.

6.4 Implementation of Survival Skills

Survival skills are the building blocks of resilience and self-sufficiency in the wasteland. Mastering these essential abilities will empower you to navigate any environment and overcome even the most daunting challenges.

Shelter building is a critical survival skill, providing protection from the elements and potential threats. Learn to construct sturdy shelters using available materials and techniques suited to your surroundings, whether it's a rudimentary lean-to or a fortified bunker.

Fire making is another invaluable skill, serving multiple purposes such as warmth, light, signaling, and purifying water. Understand the principles of fire building, including fuel selection, ignition methods, and fire safety.

Water purification is vital for ensuring a safe and reliable supply of drinking water. Familiarize yourself with various purification techniques, including boiling, filtration, and chemical treatment, to eliminate contaminants and waterborne pathogens.

Foraging for food is an essential skill in the wasteland. Develop the ability to identify edible plants, track and hunt game, and safely scavenge for non-perishable food items. Understanding food preservation methods such as drying, smoking, and pickling will further extend the longevity of your food supply.

Through hands-on practice and immersive training exercises, you will hone these critical survival skills, building the confidence and proficiency needed to thrive in any environment.

6.5 Security Measures and Threat Mitigation

In the hostile landscape of the wasteland, security is paramount. Implementing robust security measures is crucial for protecting your team and mitigating potential threats.

Begin by conducting a comprehensive threat assessment, identifying vulnerabilities in your current security posture. This may include evaluating the strength of your shelter's defenses, analyzing potential entry points for hostile forces, or monitoring for signs of dangerous wildlife in the area.

Once you have identified potential threats, implement defensive measures to fortify your position. This could involve setting up perimeter defenses, establishing strategic observation points or lookout posts, and creating physical barriers or fortifications to deter or delay potential attackers.

Develop clear protocols for threat detection, response, and escalation, ensuring that every team member understands their role and responsibilities in the event of an attack or security breach. Regular drills and simulations will help reinforce these protocols, fostering a culture of preparedness and rapid response.

Remember, in the ever-changing landscape of the wasteland, complacency can be deadly. Maintain constant vigilance, regularly reassessing your security measures and adapting them to evolving threats and circumstances.

6.6 Exfiltration to Base

Surviving in the wasteland is a continuous journey, often necessitating the relocation of your team to a new, more secure location or a return to your primary base of operations. Successful exfiltration is critical for ensuring the safety and long-term survival of your group.

6.6.1 Route Selection and Planning

When planning an exfiltration, begin by carefully analyzing the terrain features and potential obstacles along your intended route. Identify safe passages, potential choke points, and areas that may require specialized equipment or techniques for traversal.

Factor in the distance, estimated travel time, and resource requirements for the journey, ensuring that your team is adequately prepared with food, water, and essential supplies. Consider establishing cache points along the route, where additional resources or emergency provisions can be stored for contingency purposes.

6.6.2 Security and Reconnaissance

Before embarking on your exfiltration, conduct thorough security sweeps and reconnaissance along the planned route. Identify potential threats or hazards, such as hostile survivor groups, zombie hordes, or environmental dangers, and adjust your plans accordingly.

Establish overwatch positions and early warning systems to detect and respond to potential threats during the exfiltration process. This may involve deploying scouts, setting up observation posts, or utilizing technological aids like motion sensors or surveillance drones.

6.6.3 Operational Timelines and Coordination

Effective exfiltration requires precise coordination and adherence to operational timelines. Establish a clear timeline for each phase of the exfiltration, including departure, checkpoints, and arrival at the destination.

Assign specific roles and responsibilities to each team member, ensuring that everyone understands their tasks and the importance of their role in the overall operation. Maintain open communication channels and situational awareness throughout the exfiltration process, allowing for real-time updates and adjustments as needed.

Remember, the key to a successful exfiltration is adaptability. Be prepared to adjust your plans based on changing conditions or emerging threats, always prioritizing the safety and well-being of your team.

Quarry: Exfiltration

With the scavengers and their precious haul secured inside the ORP's perimeter, Sierra passed the word to Sam, "Initiate break-away!"

The defense had bought them time, dropping enough of the horde to stave off immediate over-running. But sooner or later, the sheer weight of numbers would force Sierra's outnumbered teams to withdraw fully.

Under Dakota's covering barrage, directing Parker and the other firers to continually re-supply new safe-lanes, the joined scavenger and security elements were able to break physical contact. They fell back in an organized, metered manner down their identified exfiltration path.

The horde pursued relentlessly, but Sam's rear guard was able to continually default in an economical, retrograde action with every fallback drill covered by Alex's sniper overwatch. Finally, they reached safety as the shambling masses finally lost their trail.

6.7 Adaptation to Changing Conditions

The wasteland is a dynamic and unpredictable environment, where conditions can change rapidly and without warning. To survive and thrive in this ever-evolving landscape, adaptability is essential.

Remain vigilant and responsive to changes in environmental conditions, such as shifts in weather patterns, natural disasters, or the emergence of new environmental hazards. Be prepared to adjust your shelter, clothing, and resource management strategies accordingly.

Social dynamics within your group or encounters with other survivor groups may also necessitate adaptations. Foster an environment of open communication and collaboration, allowing for the exchange of ideas and strategies to address evolving challenges.

Logistical considerations, such as supply chain disruptions or equipment failures, can also impact your survival efforts. Be proactive in identifying alternative solutions, exploring new resource acquisition methods, or improvising with available materials.

Continuous reassessment of your situation is key to staying ahead of potential problems. Regularly evaluate your plans and strategies, seeking opportunities for improvement or optimization. Embrace change as an opportunity for growth and evolution, rather than a hindrance to your survival efforts.

6.8 Communication and Coordination

Effective communication and coordination are vital for survival in the hostile environment of the wasteland. By fostering a culture of collaboration and teamwork, you can maximize efficiency, safety, and the overall chances of success for your group.

6.8.1 Establishing Communication Protocols

Begin by establishing clear communication protocols within your team. Designate primary and secondary communication channels, such as radio frequencies or visual signals, to ensure redundancy and maintain connectivity in case of equipment failure or interference.

Develop codes, encryption methods, and specialized signals to protect sensitive information and prevent interception by hostile parties. Ensure that all team members are familiar with these protocols and can communicate effectively using the established methods.

6.8.2 Assigning Roles and Responsibilities

Clearly define roles and responsibilities within your team, leveraging the unique strengths and capabilities of each individual. Assign tasks based on expertise and experience, ensuring that critical functions are covered and redundancies are in place.

Establish a clear chain of command and decision-making process, allowing for efficient and effective leadership during operations. Encourage open communication and information sharing, fostering a collaborative environment where everyone's input is valued and considered.

6.8.3 Fostering Teamwork and Collaboration

Building a strong sense of teamwork and mutual trust is essential for survival in the wasteland. Encourage open communication and information sharing among team members, promoting a culture of accountability and support.

Foster an environment of respect and understanding, acknowledging the unique perspectives and experiences of each individual. Celebrate successes as a team, and approach challenges with a collaborative mindset, seeking input and solutions from all members.

Regular team-building exercises and shared experiences can strengthen the bonds between team members, fostering a sense of camaraderie and unity in the face of adversity.

6.9 Training and Preparedness

Preparation is the key to survival in the post-apocalyptic world. Through structured training programs and practical exercises, you can build and maintain proficiency in the essential survival skills and techniques required to navigate the challenges of the wasteland.

Develop a comprehensive training curriculum that covers all aspects of survival, from basic skills like shelter building and fire making to advanced tactics for threat mitigation and exfiltration. Regularly assess your team's strengths and weaknesses, tailoring the training program to address any gaps or areas for improvement.

Conduct regular training sessions and exercises that simulate real-world scenarios your team may encounter in the wasteland. These immersive experiences will not only reinforce learned skills but also foster a mindset of readiness and adaptability.

Encourage cross-training among team members, ensuring that everyone has a basic understanding of various survival techniques and can step in to fulfill different roles as needed. This approach promotes flexibility and resilience within your group, reducing the impact of potential personnel losses or injuries.

Continuous training and preparedness are vital for maintaining a state of operational readiness. Regularly review and update your training protocols, incorporating lessons learned from previous missions and adapting to emerging threats or environmental changes in the wasteland.

6.10 Handling Wounded Personnel

In the unforgiving landscape of the wasteland, injuries and casualties are an unfortunate reality. Having a well-defined plan for handling wounded personnel can mean the difference between life and death for both the injured and the rest of your team.

6.10.1 Triage and Casualty Assessment

Establish clear triage procedures to prioritize the treatment and evacuation of casualties based on the severity of their wounds or injuries. Train your team to quickly assess casualties, evaluating signs of life, excessive bleeding, and breathing issues.

Determine transportation needs based on the condition of the wounded, identifying those who can walk or be carried, and those who require improvised litters or stretchers for evacuation.

6.10.2 Evacuation Protocols

Develop comprehensive evacuation protocols to ensure the safe and efficient extraction of wounded personnel. Plan extraction routes and fallback positions in advance, considering factors such as terrain, potential threats, and the availability of transportation resources.

Assign specific roles and responsibilities to team members during evacuation operations, including security elements to provide cover and support, medics to administer first aid, and designated carriers to transport immobile casualties.

6.10.3 Infection Monitoring

In a world overrun by the undead, the risk of infection from zombie bites or other contamination is ever-present. Implement strict protocols for monitoring team members for signs of infection, such as fever, chills, aggression, or other behavioral changes.

Establish quarantine procedures for potentially infected individuals, isolating them from the rest of the group to prevent further spread of the infection. Develop clear guidelines for respectful termination if an individual becomes fully infected, ensuring the safety of the team while maintaining human dignity.

6.11 Leave No Survivor Behind?

One of the most challenging decisions in the wasteland is whether to leave behind a critically wounded or infected team member for the sake of the group's survival. While the instinct to never abandon a comrade is admirable, the harsh realities of the post-apocalyptic world may force you to make heartbreaking choices.

6.11.1 Weighing Risks vs. Rewards

When faced with the dilemma of evacuating a wounded or infected team member, carefully assess the potential risks and rewards. Consider the likelihood of mission failure or increased danger to the rest of the team if you attempt to extract the casualty.

Evaluate the drain on resources and the team's ability to continue moving and evading threats while transporting or protecting the injured individual. Factor in the chances of the casualty's survival based on the severity of their condition and the resources available for treatment.

6.11.2 Heartbreaking Decisions

Sometimes, the tough decision may be to leave behind a critically wounded or infected team member, prioritizing the survival of the group over the individual. This decision should never be made lightly and should consider all alternatives and the chances of the casualty's survival.

If the decision is made to leave someone behind, provide for their final dignity and comfort, administering mercy if necessary to prevent a fate worse than death. Ensure that any personal effects or messages are respectfully handled and delivered to loved ones, if possible.

6.11.3 Accountability

Document the reasons and circumstances of any decision to leave a team member behind, ensuring a clear record of the thought process and factors considered. Notify higher command or base personnel of the situation and any casualties sustained as soon as possible.

Be prepared to justify your actions and decisions when challenged, providing a thorough accounting of the circumstances, the options evaluated, and the rationale behind your choices. Maintain detailed logs, recordings, or written accounts that can substantiate the necessity of the decision.

While such choices are never easy, maintaining a clear chain of accountability is critical. It allows for an objective review process, learning from past incidents, and implementing improved procedures to minimize future loss of life in similar scenarios.

However, accountability extends beyond documenting tactical decisions. Address the psychological impacts within your team through counseling, guided discussions, and fostering an environment where the emotional weight of such actions can be processed in a healthy manner. Provide respites, rotation schedules, and mental health support to prevent an accumulation of trauma or moral injury among survivors.

Ultimately, the life-or-death decisions made in the wasteland will burden even the strongest leaders and teams. Maintaining a robust accountability process, both for documenting decisions and addressing the residual inner conflicts, is essential for preserving the resilience, effectiveness and humanity of your team in the face of the harshest sacrifices. The accountability light must remain burning, even in the darkest hours.

6.12 Post-Mission Activities

The scavenging mission doesn't truly end until all personnel, equipment, and acquired resources have been properly accounted for and reintegrated back at your base of operations. Crucial post-mission activities must be conducted to ensure operational security, replenish for the next mission, and review lessons learned.

6.12.1 Inventorying Scavenged Supplies

As the team returns from the wasteland, a thorough inventory must be conducted of all scavenged supplies and resources:

(1) Unload and Consolidate: Carefully unpack and consolidate all acquired items into a central collection point.

(2) Inspection and Cataloging: Inspect each item's condition, quantity, and document it into the master inventory logs.

(3) Test/Evaluation of Equipment: Any recovered equipment, weapons, vehicles etc. should be test fired and evaluated.

(4) Secure Storage: Properly stored and secured all reusable items in designated supply warehouses or armories.

6.12.2 Personnel Search and Screening

To prevent any supplies or restricted items from being pocketed, all returning personnel must submit to a thorough search:

(1) Personal Belongings Checked: All packs, pouches, and personal carry items are physically inspected.

(2) **Pat Down Frisk:** Members of the inspection team conduct a thorough pat down of each person.

(3) **Substance Screening**: If indicated, personnel may be screened for exposure to chemicals or biological agents.

(4) **Separate Holding Areas:** Those still requiring additional screening are segregated to a holding area.

6.12.3 Medical Screening and Treatment

Anyone injured or exposed to potential contamination during the mission must receive medical evaluation:

(1) **Decontamination:** If exposure is suspected, team members go through full decontamination upon return.

(2) **Triage and Stabilization**: Medics conduct in-processing triage to treat any injuries or illness.

(3) **Medical Examination:** A more thorough examination by a physician is conducted on any still requiring treatment.

(4) **Observation Period:** Those exposed may be held for a period to monitor for any potential delayed symptoms.

6.12.4 Mission Debrief and After-Action Review

A formal debrief is required to capture lessons learned and improve future operations:

(1) Personnel Interviews: An impartial debrief officer interviews all members about what transpired during the mission.

(2) **Fact-Finding Investigation:** Any incidents, security breaches or failures are investigated.

(3) **After-Action Review (AAR):** Leadership conducts an in-depth AAR to review what went right/wrong and needed changes.

(4) **Integration of Lessons Learned:** Identified issues are used to update operational plans, training, and procedures.

While often overlooked, this post-mission process is vital for objectively evaluating each operation to uphold standards and maintain combat readiness. It allows areas for improvement to be identified and corrected before future missions are jeopardized.

Quarry: After Action

Immediately after the mission, when memories were still clear, Sierra added her notations to the official After-Action Review:

"Success ultimately achieved, though at cost of wounded. Key lessons included:
(1) the Value of a leader's reconnaissance in noting security requirements for establishing interlocking Fields of Fire and fallback routes prior to committing forces.
(2) Necessity of designating overwatch roles for top cover and sniper defense against hostile overrun.
(3) Being prepared for all contingencies - horde's aggressive reaction required battle drill implementation of break-away sequence before scavenging mission could be considered complete . . ."

The Battle of Quarryville showed that even for a scavenging run that initially went to plan, the unpredictable threat environment mandated forward planning and strict adherence to establishing force protection and security in any operation area. Those disciplines enabled Sierra's teams to endure hostile engagement and safely recover both personnel and critical resources to fight another day.

Conclusion

Survival in the post-apocalyptic world is not merely about enduring—it's about embracing the journey, learning from its challenges, and emerging stronger and more resilient than ever before. In this concluding chapter, we reflect on the lessons learned, celebrate the resilience of survivors, and look to the future with hope and determination.

7.1 Reflecting on the Journey

As we come to the end of this manual, take a moment to reflect on the journey you've embarked upon. From the first page to this one, we've explored the depths of survival in the post-apocalyptic world, uncovering essential strategies, skills, and insights along the way. Consider the challenges you've faced, the knowledge you've gained, and the growth you've experienced as a survivor.

7.2 Celebrating Resilience

Survivors are a testament to the resilience of the human spirit. Despite the trials and tribulations of the post-apocalyptic world, they persevere, adapt, and thrive in the face of adversity. Take a moment to celebrate your resilience and that of your fellow survivors. Recognize the strength and determination that have carried you through even the darkest of times.

7.3 Looking to the Future

While the journey may be fraught with challenges, the future holds endless possibilities. As survivors, we must look forward with hope and optimism, knowing that each day brings new opportunities for growth and renewal. Consider the path that lies ahead and the role you will play in shaping the world of tomorrow.

7.4 Expressing Gratitude

None of us can survive alone. Throughout our journey, we've relied on the support and contributions of fellow survivors, mentors, and allies who have helped us along the way. Take a moment to express gratitude for their guidance, encouragement, and friendship. Remember the bonds forged in adversity and the strength found in community.

7.5 Final Words of Wisdom

As we prepare to part ways, let us leave with a few final words of wisdom. Remember to stay vigilant, adaptable, and compassionate in all your endeavors. Never lose sight of your humanity, even in the darkest of times. And above all, never give up hope. For as long as there is life, there is the potential for a better tomorrow.

7.6 Call to Action

Our journey does not end here—it merely takes on a new form. As survivors, we have a responsibility to share our knowledge and experiences